MYSTERY AT THE
MASQUERADE

LOVE IS IN THE SALT SEA AIR— AND SO IS MURDER!

Ellery Page, aspiring screenwriter,
reigning Scrabble champion,
and occasionally clueless owner
of the village's only mystery bookstore,
the Crow's Nest,
is both flattered and bemused
when he's invited to the Marauder's Masquerade,
the best and biggest social event of the season
in the quaint seaside village of Pirate's Cove.

As his relationship with Police Chief Carson
seems to be dead in the water,
Ellery is grateful for a little flattering attention
from the village's most eligible bachelor,
but any hopes of romance hit the shoals
when murder occurs during
the annual ghost hunt.

MYSTERY AT THE MASQUERADE

SECRETS & SCRABBLE BOOK THREE

JOSH LANYON

VELLICHOR BOOKS

An imprint of JustJoshin Publishing, Inc.

MYSTERY AT THE MASQUERADE: AN M/M COZY Mystery
(Secrets and Scrabble Book 3)
February 2021
Copyright (c) 2021 by Josh Lanyon
Edited by Keren Reed
Cover and book design by Kevin Burton Smith
All rights reserved.

ISBN: 978-1-945802-68-3
Published in the United States of America

JustJoshin Publishing, Inc.
3053 Rancho Vista Blvd.
Suite 116
Palmdale, CA 93551
www.joshlanyon.com

This is a work of fiction. Any resemblance to persons living or dead is entirely coincidental.

To Kevin, my saint in tough guy's clothing.

Upon one summer's morning,
I carefully did stray
Down by the Walls of Wapping,
Where I met a sailor gay
"My Jolly Sailor Bold"

CHAPTER ONE

"**B**urglary?" Ellery asked doubtfully.

"It looks like it." Jack selected a French fry, considered it, folded it into his mouth.

They were having lunch on the outside patio at the Gull's Wing Café. The patio was surrounded by July's summer visitors to Pirate's Cove and, yes, gulls. A lot of seagulls swooping in for the bites of burger and fried fish tourists offered up, despite the forest-worth of signs requesting people NOT to feed the birds.

"In *your* town?" Ellery joked.

Jack's grin was sardonic. "I know. I must be losing my touch."

Once upon a time, and not so long ago, Ellery would have made some little jokey, flirty comment about Jack's touch, but they had recently decided to, er, hold the position. The position being friends. Strictly friends. Without benefits.

Well, no, because there were definitely benefits to being friends. Ellery was glad they were friends.

Sure, he would have liked to see where things might have gone with Jack, but he was a guy who could take no for an answer.

"Why do you think it took the owners so long to report the break-in?" Ellery asked, staring down a particularly large gull watching him from the white railing.

"Nobody noticed. The burglar climbed vines on a trellis and got in through an upstairs window. There isn't any staff when the Bloodworths aren't staying on the island. The caretaker is about a hundred years old."

"Was the window unlocked?"

"Nope. They had to break in."

A gull landed on the pebble top table and fastened its beady gaze on Ellery's grinder. Jack snapped, "*Hey.*"

The gull jumped, offered an affronted squawk, and took flight, wings beating the sparkling air. A few of the other diners—including Ellery—jumped as well. Jack's *hey* was pretty commanding, even when it was off-duty. Not that Buck Island's police chief was ever really off-duty.

Ellery said, "Maybe you should cut down on the caffeine, Jack. Just sayin'."

Jack muttered, "It takes all winter to train them not to beg, and the first week of summer, it's like living through the movie *The Birds*."

"Mm-hm."

Ellery was mostly kidding, though Jack did seem a little wound-up lately.

Jack grimaced acknowledgment. "Maybe."

"So what did the burglar get away with?"

"Several thousand dollars' worth of antique sterling silver. Picture frames, trays, serving sets and, of course, a whole lot of silverware."

"Small items easily disposed of?" Five months ago, Ellery had inherited the island's only mystery bookshop, and he was now something of an armchair detective. Not that it took a detective, armchair or otherwise, to draw that conclusion.

"Correct."

Ellery said bracingly, "You'll get 'em. It's an island. People talk. Someone knows who your bad guy or bad guys are."

"Or bad girls." Jack chose another French fry. Sunlight gleamed off his wedding band.

Ellery wasn't sure when Jack had started wearing his ring again—but then, he couldn't pinpoint when Jack had stopped wearing his ring. He had not worn it on their sole "date," but it had reappeared in the weeks since.

Honestly? Better not to try to analyze what was happening there.

But it *was* confusing sometimes. Sometimes like now, when Jack's gaze would catch his own and linger, linger, until Jack finally looked away. Or sometimes Ellery would glance up and find Jack studying him as though Ellery presented a puzzle Jack just couldn't figure out.

His thoughts broke off as a woman sitting a couple of tables away from their own suddenly squealed, "NO! NO WAY!"

She plucked a small black envelope from her companion, tore it open, and pulled out the small card inside. A wisp of tissue paper drifted on the breeze and was snatched up by a kamikaze seagull.

The other woman laughed, watching her friend, and then winced when the first woman lightly bonked her on the head with the card.

"I don't believe it!" the first woman exclaimed. "Why *you*?"

The second woman laughed again. People at neighboring tables also laughed.

"What the what?" Ellery glanced at Jack, who was watching the exchange with a resigned expression.

"It's the same every year."

"What's the same?"

"The countdown for the last golden tickets to the chocolate factory."

Ellery always found Jack's familiarity with children's literary classics kind of charming, but this time he didn't get the reference.

"Huh?"

"The hullabaloo over who rates an invite to the Marauder's Masquerade and who doesn't."

Hullabaloo. What a great word. Ellery made a mental note, said patiently, "I think you think that I know what you're talking about."

Jack looked surprised, started to speak, but was interrupted by the crackle of the radio mic on his shoulder.

"Chief? Chief?" cackled Officer Martin. "Are you there, Chief?"

Jack sighed, threw Ellery a look of apology, and rose from the table.

* * * * *

"The Marauder's Masquerade is one of the biggest social events of the season. Certainly, the most prestigious." Nora Sweeny, head of the now-defunct Pirate's Cove Historical Society, and Ellery's assistant at the Crow's Nest, was talking in an animated fashion. Ostensibly to Ellery, but really to anyone in listening distance.

"That's interesting," Ellery said absently. "So it's a ball? A masquerade ball?" He was mostly being polite, his real focus on shelving new stock from the morning's shipment from HarperCollins.

"Yes. Exactly. A gala ball and ghost hunt."

"Ghost hunt?" *That* caught Ellery's attention. He wasn't much for gala balls, but a ghost hunt? That sounded like fun.

"Yes. The ghost hunt is the main event."

"Whose ghost is being hunted?"

Nora's face screwed up in thought. She was a small, slight, seventy-something with the energy of a woman half her age and the inbred fortitude of seven generations of staunch New Englanders. "There's a difference of opinion there. Some claim the ghost of Tom Blood walks among the gravestones and statues of his descendants. That seems rather unlikely, as Captain Blood went down with his crew when the *Blood Red Rose* was lost at sea."

"If it's not Captain Blood, then who is it?"

Nora loved mysteries. Especially the real-life historical ones. It was safe to assume she would have a theory.

"His bride. Maria Catalina Isabella de Fontana. A seventeen-year-old Spanish noblewoman Blood abducted and then wed—supposedly with her full and willing consent. Which, given her age, doesn't mean much. When his ship went down, she threw herself into the sea."

"That seems to happen a lot on this island," Ellery commented. "I'm starting to wonder if there's something in the water."

Watson, Ellery's six-month-old black spaniel-mix puppy, waddled over and curled up between Ellery's feet with a groan reminiscent of an elderly man lowering himself into his easy chair. Ellery had nearly tripped over Watson twice that morning already, but Watson seemed to be suffering a mild case of separation anxiety.

"Has Ellery been invited to the Marauder's Masquerade?" Mrs. Clarence demanded, dropping her pile of books onto the counter for Nora to ring up.

Ellery laughed at the idea.

"Not yet," Nora said cheerfully, grabbing the first of Mrs. Clarence's paperbacks and ringing it up. Mrs. Clarence was a fan of spy and espionage books. "I'm sure he will be."

"Why would I be?" Ellery objected.

Mrs. Clarence said, "Everyone who's anyone is invited. Isn't that right, dear?"

Nora nodded. "Exactly right."

"I repeat, why would *I* be invited?"

The ladies ignored him. Nora beamed at Mrs. Clarence. "Have you received your invite, dear?"

"Me?" Mrs. Clarence chuckled. She was somewhere in her late sixties, very tall, very blonde, sleek and surprisingly stylish for one of Pirate Cove's matrons. "Oh, I don't think I'm on the Bloodworths' social radar."

"You never know, Edna. Nora's been invited to the Masquerade many times." Mrs. Nelson's voice floated from the Cozy Mystery section. Mrs. Nelson was another of Ellery's regular customers, although maybe *customer* wasn't the exact word, given that she returned as many books as she kept. She was a member of Tuesday night's Silver Sleuths Book Club.

Thanks largely to Nora's tireless efforts and, probably, her standing as one of Pirate Cove's best-informed gossips, the Crow's Nest was becoming one of the village's unofficial community centers.

Nora looked regretful. "Not since I wrote that biography of Tom Blood for the Historical Society's newsletter."

"Ah." Mrs. Clarence looked sympathetic. "I've always thought Marguerite lacked a sense of humor."

The invisible Mrs. Nelson concurred.

Nora sighed. "It's a shame. The spread they put on is magnificent. Nothing less than magnificent. But I refuse to whitewash history. Not for all the crab puffs in New England."

Ellery faced out the final book, and wheeled the empty book cart back to the counter, followed by Watson. He reached the counter just as Mr. Starling, another of the Crow's Nest regulars, joined Nora and Mrs. Clarence at the cash register. Ellery regretted ever bringing up the topic of the Marauder's Masquerade.

"There's some talk the Masquerade was nearly canceled this year," Mr. Starling announced. "That's why the invitations went out so late."

"Oh!" exclaimed Mrs. Clarence. "That would be the first time in nearly eighty years."

"No, dear," Mrs. Nelson called. "They didn't hold the Masquerade during the war."

"Where did you hear such a thing, Stanley?" Nora no doubt felt she had been scooped.

Mr. Starling's news even brought Mrs. Nelson, broad and stalwart as a schooner, sailing out from behind the tall shelves. "Are you sure it's true?"

Mr. Starling nodded solemnly. "I have it on the best authority."

Nora's gray eyes narrowed. "I suppose you mean Jonas Landry. How someone that loose-lipped has survived as a lawyer for fifty years boggles the mind." She glanced at Ellery, read his expression correctly, and blushed.

"Have you been invited to the Masquerade, Mr. Starling?" Ellery threw over his shoulder, pushing the book cart into his office.

Mr. Starling made a noise that around the holidays would be classified as *bah-humbug*. "I have no interest in that kind of nonsense."

The doorbell chimed, and a group of young women wearing sunglasses and toting shopping bags pushed inside. Tourists. Which meant they might actually sell some books that afternoon. Except... The day trippers took one look at the club meeting taking place at the sales desk, exchanged looks, and backed right out again.

Ellery swallowed his disappointment. It was hard to find the right balance. He didn't want to offend his regulars, but the Crow's Nest needed more business to survive. A lot more business.

Meanwhile...

"Yes, that *would* explain why the invitations are going out so late," Mrs. Nelson was musing. "She handed over a single paperback to Nora. "I'll take this one, Nora."

"You've already purchased and returned that one twice," Nora informed her.

"Have I?" Mrs. Nelson looked astonished. She studied the cartoony figures on the bright pastel cover. "Oh, I believe you're right. It was the pastry chef, wasn't it? Ellery, you're really going to have to order more stock."

"No way," Ellery said. "Not until every single title of existing stock has been sold."

The four of them gaped at him, and Ellery laughed. "Kidding. I just shelved a whole new shipment."

Mrs. Nelson shook her head. She said to Nora, "He's such an odd boy, isn't he, dear?"

"But charming," Mrs. Clarence put in.

This was too much for Mr. Starling. He grumbled something and headed for the door.

"Will we see you tonight, Stanley?" Nora called.

Mr. Starling waved his hand and growled something unintelligible. The bell on the door chimed cheerfully as he departed. The ladies at the counter smiled at each other.

"You must join our book club, dear," Mrs. Nelson told Mrs. Clarence. "We're reading Diana Killian's *Corpse Pose.*"

"*Still?*" Ellery said. "Weren't you reading that last month?"

Nora and Mrs. Nelson stared blankly at him, and Ellery put his hands up in surrender. "Okay. Whatever. So long as you're enjoying yourselves."

Nora smiled approvingly and then beamed in welcome as another customer made her way diffidently to the counter.

"What have we here?" Nora held up the book to her eyeline to gain a closer look. "Ah, Brandon Abbott's last book. Very good. His books have been selling like hotcakes since…" Her gaze slid to Ellery. "Since the dreadful tragedy!" Nora finished cheerfully.

Ellery sighed and went to tear down the signage from last weekend's sale.

CHAPTER TWO

A silver sliver of crescent moon seemed to have hooked itself on one of the twin conical towers of Captain's Seat when Ellery arrived home that Tuesday evening.

Ellery parked in the drive and let Watson out to run around chasing varmints both real and imagined.

Arf. Arf. Arf.

Watson's piercing bark echoed off the stone drive and towers as he raced from flower bed to steps and back again.

Ellery propped his hands on his hips and drew in deep breaths of cool evening air. The soothing scents of the warm meadow and ocean drifted on the summer breeze. Lights twinkled through the trees. Many of the island's summer homes were occupied now, though Ellery's home was still quite isolated from its nearest neighbors.

Home was kind of a weird word for Captain's Seat.

The decaying Dutch Renaissance style mansion Ellery had inherited from his Great-great-great-aunt Eudora had been commissioned in the eighteenth century by the famous pirate hunter Captain Horatio Page.

Why a pirate hunter would decide to settle down on an island that had served as a pirate sanctuary for a couple of centuries was a question for the ages. Safe to say, the old boy had not been easily intimidated.

Captain's Seat boasted—or maybe *confessed* was a better word—six bedrooms and seven baths. The bedrooms were spacious, even cavernous, from a heating-bill standpoint. Luckily, each bedroom had its own fireplace. Along with all the bedrooms and fireplaces came a grand foyer, a great hall, a gallery, a drawing room, a library, a game room (sadly, popular games in Captain Page's day had not included Scrabble), a pantry, and a wine cellar that could easily double for a dungeon.

When Ellery wasn't working at the bookshop—which, granted, wasn't often—he spent his time renovating Captain's Seat. Given the years and years of neglect and his own lack of experience in home renovation, it was beginning to look like restoring the mansion would be his life's mission. His undertaking had been made even more difficult by a fire on the second level that had happened in June.

Sometimes Jack joined him in the home repairs. Jack's boyhood summers had been spent working for his father's construction company, and he was an expert at home improvements. With Jack's help, Ellery had managed to repair most of the upstairs smoke damage and refinish the railings and bannister of the tall, graceful staircase in the formal entry hall.

Jack seemed to find the work relaxing, and they'd spent many pleasant days sanding, painting, hammering. Sometimes they talked, and sometimes they just worked in companionable silence. Sometimes they shared a meal. Sometimes they didn't.

Ellery let Watson run himself out, and then he unlocked the front door, stepped over the scattered envelopes and flyers that had arrived in the day's mail, and flipped on the newly rewired chandelier. Light sparkled off the dangling crystals and flickered like butterflies against the pearl-pale walls.

Watson ran to pick up his favorite stuffed-toy hedgehog, which he proceeded to toss in the air.

Ellery laughed, grabbed the hedgehog, and pitched it up the staircase. Watson raced to retrieve it. They played that game until even Watson tired, and then Ellery went into the kitchen to fix their supper.

Finding the abandoned puppy on that lonely stretch of road between Pirate's Cove and Captain's Seat had been one of the best things that had happened to Ellery. The pup's lively, loving personality had changed the whole atmosphere at Captain's Seat. Plus, taking care of Watson provided unexpected structure to his life, which had previously consisted almost entirely of working at the bookshop and working on home renovations.

He opened a packet of fresh dog food for Watson, dumped the meat and veggies into Watson's metal bowl, and placed the bowl on the floor for the puppy, who was hopping up and down as though he hadn't eaten in weeks. The truth was, it was all Ellery could do to keep his customers from slipping Watson treats throughout the day.

He watched, brows raised, as Watson dived nose first into his bowl, making sounds more similar to a piglet than a puppy, then set about figuring his own supper.

There was still a decent portion of the tuna casserole Nora had made him last Friday. Nora's tuna casserole was in a class of its own. Maybe it was the fresh tuna, maybe it was the potato chips, but it was as delicious as it was hearty.

While the casserole heated, Ellery went to fetch his mail, sorting through the inevitable pile of catalogs and consigning most of it to the recycling bin. Great-great-great-aunt Eudora had apparently been on every mailing list in the world (surely Auntie E. had not been a regular customer of Frederick's of Hollywood?!).

He regarded a black envelope with a showy red seal with resignation. Another "special" credit-card offer, no doubt. He turned the envelope over. His name was hand-printed in elegant gold lettering.

He looked at the seal again and realized it was real wax and embossed with what looked like a sailing ship. A pirate ship?

"No. Way."

Watson, noisily scooting his dish back and forth across the newly refinished floor, ignored him.

Ellery ripped open the fancy black envelope, withdrew the fancy black card inside—a slip of tissue fluttered down—and flipped open the card.

You are invited to the

MARAUDER'S MASQUERADE

Honoring Captain Thomas Blood

Saturday, July 10, at 7:00 PM

Bloodworth Manor House

The Bluffs

Pirate's Cove, RI 02807

COSTUME AND MASK REQUIRED

A handwritten note at the bottom of the card read: *Sincere apologies for the late notice, but your attendance is greatly desired.*

"Greatly desired," murmured Ellery. He didn't get that a lot these days. He was both flattered and baffled.

The microwave dinged, breaking the spell. Ellery tossed the card to the table and went to get his casserole.

While he ate, he browsed the 1923 edition of *Pirates of New England* he'd found in Great-great-great-aunt Eudora's considerable (and considerably dusty) library.

Thomas Bloodworth was one of the so-called "Pirate's Eight" of Buck Island. These were eight pirates of the late sixteenth or early seventeenth century, who had made the island their home base and built substantial fortifications or "castles," most of which still stood to that day. Not much was known about most of this pirate fraternity, but Bloodworth—or, as he was known professionally, Captain Blood—had a better PR machine behind him. He was still viewed as one of the "gentlemen pirates" of the seventeenth century.

According to *Pirates of New England*, he was born the bastard son of a names-changed-to-protect-the-innocent English lord, and had chosen adventure over priesthood. Which, seeing the way things turned out, shouldn't have come as a surprise to anyone. The young Thomas had given up a commission in the Royal Navy and turned his talents to marauding and murder. He was a very successful pirate and might even have lived to retire comfortably had his ship, the *Blood Red Rose*, not been destroyed in a hurricane off the coast of Buck Island.

Ellery studied the history book's rather gorgeous illustration of Captain Blood. It looked like something N.C. Wyeth might have come up with for *Treasure Island*.

No question, Blood had cut a dashing figure. The reality would no doubt have been a lot different. Reality always was. But he was looking forward to seeing the results of all that ill-gotten gain—and how the bloodline (no pun intended) had fared through the centuries.

When Ellery opened the door to the Crow's Nest the next morning, the first thing he spotted was the glass-encased complete pirate costume from Skull House. It was the only item Ellery had removed from the old mansion. The pirate costume was a huge hit with visitors to the bookshop.

He nodded pleasantly to the resin skeleton he'd privately named Rupert. Rupert grinned hollowly back, and Ellery set about opening the shop for the day. Or, in other words, making coffee.

He had come to love the old bookshop with its burnished wooden floors and big bay windows with their view of the harbor. Tidy shelves stacked with hundreds, no, thousands of stories of mystery and intrigue and adventure, and, yes, even romance. Something for everyone. Everyone who loved a mystery, at least.

The morning light reflected off the row of ships' lanterns lining the back wall, sending flashes of blue and green washing across the timbered ceiling and the vintage seascape oil paintings.

He had not inherited this little jewel. In fact, he'd inherited something a lot closer to a haunted warehouse full of cobwebs, moldering books, and dusty bric-a-brac. Also the odd lethal weapon, one of which still lay in PICO PD's evidence room. Ellery had spent a lot of time painting walls, washing windows, sanding floors, and polishing furniture, in an effort to make the bookshop a cozy and inviting space, and for the most part he had succeeded.

The Crow's Nest would never be mistaken for a cash cow, but at least during the summer months they were holding their own.

"Guess what?" Ellery said when Nora came in a short while later.

"You've been invited to the Marauder's Masquerade," Nora said.

Ellery closed his mouth.

"Sorry, dearie," Nora said. "But didn't I tell you?"

"You missed your calling, Nora. You should have been a fortune teller."

Nora preened. "It doesn't take special powers to recognize the inevitable. Obviously, you would be invited."

"Well, it wasn't obvious to me. Anyway—"

"Oh, you *have* to go!" Once again Nora seemed to read his mind.

"If I can figure out some kind of costume, I will. It has to be pirate gear, right?"

"Seventeenth or eighteenth century finery. That won't be a problem," Nora assured him.

Ellery raised an eyebrow. "It won't?"

"No, no."

They were interrupted by the first customer of the day. And it really was a customer! A middle-aged man looking for something on the lines of Tripp Ellis.

Nora steered him to Nelson DeMille, James Rollins, and John McKinna.

The customer bought four paperbacks, and Ellery and Nora high-fived each other as the front door swung closed behind him.

Later, when Ellery was setting up the clearance table, he said, "I was reading about Tom Blood last night."

"Oh yes?"

"The Gentleman Pirate according to *Pirates of New England*."

Nora sniffed. She took a dim view of "prettified" history, which, in her opinion, was any history book written before 1975. "He could have been worse, I suppose. You'll see his portrait when you attend the masquerade. It hangs in the great hall. It was painted by Augustine Clement."

"There's a reproduction in the book."

"That's right. Well, handsome is as handsome does." Nora finished dusting the Riker display with its trove of shells, seahorses, and starfish. She stepped back to admire her handiwork.

"Has the wreck of the *Blood Red Rose* ever been discovered?"

"No."

"Do you think the legends are true? That she sank off the coast of Buck Island?"

"It's very possible. Just because she hasn't been found doesn't mean she isn't there."

"Are the Bloodworths actually direct descendants of Tom Blood?"

"Oh yes. There's no mistaking that nose. Or those eyes."

"Huh?"

"There's a distinct familial resemblance undiluted through the generations. You'll see when you view the portrait. They used to call Marguerite the Pirate's Granddaughter. She bears such a strong physical resemblance to Tom Blood. Physical and…"

Nora didn't finish the thought.

"And?" Ellery inquired.

Nora said vaguely, "I hate to spread gossip, dearie."

Since when? Ellery managed to keep that to himself. "Of course," he said gravely. "Why, it's been nearly a week since your last contribution to the Gossip Jar."

Nora brightened. "That's true. I'm a changed woman."

Ellery teased, "Well, don't change too much. Everything I know about Buck Island, I learned from you."

"Well, in the interests of broadening your historical knowledge of the island, it was Tom Blood who came up with the idea of building the system of tunnels beneath Pirate's Cove. He was very much involved in deciding how the island would be governed. Up until Tom Blood, the island had no political infrastructure. It was every man or pirate for himself. Tom

Blood convinced his fellow marauders that it would be to their benefit to put hand-picked representatives into key positions to deal with the pesky Royal Navy or any mainland excise men who showed up. His name appears on the village charter."

"So…one of our founding fathers?"

"Ha!" Nora considered, admitted, "But yes. Frankly, he was."

"I read that Blood used to anchor his ship in a hidden cove—although, why? Since the whole island was a pirate hideout?"

"That's true. The *Blood Red Rose* used to lie anchored in the cove beneath Seal Point. That was later on. After he had fallen out with some of his fellow pirates."

"I see. And how can there be descendants of Tom Blood when his bride threw herself in the ocean?"

"Maria Catalina Isabella de Fontana was Captain Blood's *second* bride. Assuming he actually wed the poor child. He was already married, of course, and had several children with Eleanor Gilbert."

Ellery was unsure if Nora meant Eleanor Gilbert was the first Mrs. Captain Blood or an additional dalliance. Not that the first Mrs. Captain Blood would be a *dalliance*.

In any case, the subject changed as the bell on the front door jingled cheerfully, and Nora's niece, Nan Sweeny, stepped inside. "It's going to be a hot one!" she announced.

Nan owned the Seacrest Inn and was Pirate Cove's acting mayor until the next special election could be held—which it seemed no one was in a hurry to do. Like her aunt, Nan was short, slim, and a bundle of energy. Her hair was worn in a glossy brown bob, and her eyes were bright with humor and intelligence.

"Morning!" Ellery said.

Nan looked from Ellery to Nora. "Did Auntie tell you?"

"Tell me what?" Ellery glanced warily at Nora.

"I didn't have a chance, dearie," Nora apologized.

"Ellery, we want you to be Mr. April."

"Mr...."

"April!" Nan beamed. "For the village calendar."

Ellery probably looked only more puzzled because Nora told Nan, "He's using a Norman Rockwell freebie his insurance agent mailed us."

"Oh *no*." Nan looked shocked.

"If he knew better..." Nora prodded.

Nan took the hint. "Right! Well, Ellery, every year the town council commissions a calendar for the next year, featuring our most prominent gentlemen becomingly clad in pirate costume. The proceeds go to the widows-and-orphans fund."

"Uh-oh, did I just fall down a wormhole?" Ellery asked.

Nan laughed merrily. "Oh, I know what you're thinking. It's a little bit sexist and a little bit...um, *retro* in mindset, but it sells like fire and it's for a really good cause."

Were there really that many widows and orphans in Pirate's Cove? Sure, back in the days of Captain Blood, but *now*?

"I'm sure it is, it's just that..."

"It's an honor, dearie," Nora assured him.

"*Is* it?"

"Oh yes. Of course it is." Nora added shrewdly, "Police Chief Carson takes part every year."

"*Jack?* Jack poses for a beefcake calendar?"

"He certainly does. Well, I mean, we don't think of it as *beefcake*, but yes."

Ellery gazed doubtfully at Nan, who coaxed, "It would be so lovely if you would agree to April. You would be perfect."

"Mr. Carter has been Mr. November for the last five years," Nora chimed in.

Okay, well, Dylan would find this entire enterprise hugely amusing, so that wasn't as surprising as learning Jack was a willing victim.

Nan said, "It wouldn't take more than a couple of hours on an afternoon. And you've had modeling experience, so this would be nothing for you."

True. This was nothing he hadn't done before. In fact, he'd even modeled a child's pirate hat and eye patch for the Sears Wish Book about a million Christmases ago. A sign of things to come?

Ellery said slowly, "I guess so? Since it's for a good cause?"

"Perfect!" Nan's smile was suspiciously bright.

"Who am I replacing?" Ellery asked curiously.

Nan and Nora exchanged an indecipherable look.

"Brett Ainsley," Nan said.

The name meant nothing to Ellery, and in any case, further conversation was forestalled by the arrival of Dylan, who entered on a triumphant jangle of the doorbell.

"Yo-ho-ho. Did I hear some landlubber be needing a pirate costume for the ball on Saturday?"

"Did you?" Ellery said. "I mean, *how* did you? I only found out myself last night."

"So it's true! I knew it." Dylan, Nan, and Nora beamed at each other with satisfaction.

Ellery studied them warily. "Did one of you three—did you three wrangle an invite for me?"

"No!" Dylan put his hands up in an I'm-innocent-Your-Honor! gesture. "Of course not!"

"Because I'm pretty sure I've never met any of the Bloodworths."

Nora was shaking her head firmly. "Absolutely not, dearie. I myself am persona non grata with that crowd." She sniffed at the memory of past slights.

"Not guilty," Nan assured him.

"Then I really don't understand how or why I was invited."

Dylan protested, "What? Of course you were invited. For one thing, you're a movie star. For another, you're one of the community's business leaders."

"I'm…"

"Absolutely!" Nora said. "And don't forget—you've solved *two* murders in a matter of months. That alone makes you a celebrity within the village."

"Yeee-ah. I really don't think—"

"I have the perfect costume in mind for you," Dylan interrupted.

"What? How—"

"Dearie, we have the entire costume department of the Scallywags to choose from," Nora pointed out.

"Exactly," Dylan said. "I've been thinking about this. We have that beautiful black velvet frock coat Tom wore in *The Pirates of Penzance*."

"The one with gold braid?" Nora exclaimed. "Yes. I was thinking the same thing. I'll have to take it in a bit, but it's perfect for him! And what about the green-gold silk waistcoat with the embroidered clocks that Felix wore in *A Harlot's Progress*?"

"You read my mind," Dylan told her.

"Wait. Wait just a minute," Ellery objected. "*A*—no way do Felix and I wear the same size. He's like half of me. And *B*—are you telling me the Scallywags performed *A Harlot's Progress*?"

"No, no," Dylan said. "The town fathers would never go for that."

"Nor the town mothers," Nora added sadly.

"We did a scene during last year's Fringe Festival in Providence."

"I'll have to take the coat in and let the vest out..." Nora's thoughts were running ahead to more practical matters. "That won't be a problem. I know your size."

"You know my size? How would you know my size?"

"Dearie, I've been making costumes for the Scallywags for the last fifty years. Do you truly not believe I can size a man with a glance?"

"I truly do *not* believe that," Ellery said.

"Well, it may have taken more than a glance," Nora admitted. "But I'm quite confident I have your measure."

Ellery said to Dylan, "Why does it sound like she's talking about more than my clothes?"

"No use arguing," Dylan said jovially. "You're going to the ball, Cinderfella!"

CHAPTER THREE

"**T**his is a nice surprise," Ellery remarked, dragging out the chair across from Jack.

Jack had phoned the bookshop just as Ellery had been locking up for the day, inviting him to dinner at the pub. Ellery had accepted, left Watson with young Terry, the daughter of Sandy Morita who owned the art gallery next to the Crow's Nest, and headed for the Salty Dog.

Jack said, "I saw the lights were still on at the Crow's Nest and knew you were working late and probably hadn't stopped to eat."

Two meals together in one week? That was kind of a record, but Ellery knew not to get the wrong idea. Jack preferred to dine off-island when he was dating. This was just two pals grabbing dinner. They both frequented the Salty Dog for dinner, so why not share a table and a meal?

Ellery smiled. "You're right about that. There wasn't time today for more than a doughnut and coffee this morning. Not that I'm complaining. It's a relief to finally have some business. If the rest of the summer continues like this, we might actually be in the black by September."

Jack's brows rose. "I thought… What about Abbott's estate? Didn't everything go to you?"

"On paper. But the will is still in probate. Brandon's agent is contesting the dispensation of Brandon's literary estate. Plus, Brandon pretty much spent money as fast as he made it." Ellery shrugged. He wasn't counting on ever seeing a penny from Brandon's estate, and that was probably just as well.

"I didn't realize."

"Sure." Jack didn't realize because ever since the events of the previous month, Ellery had followed Jack's lead in keeping their conversations casual and largely impersonal. If Jack didn't ask, Ellery didn't offer.

Libby Tulley appeared at their table and requested their drink orders. A small and lively redhead, Libby was the daughter of Tom Tulley, owner and proprietor of the Salty Dog.

Ellery had got to know her pretty well during the spring production of his play *Murder Mansion*. Which, given that Libby was a teenaged girl, meant she remained a complete mystery to him and everyone else.

Ellery ordered a Tipsy Mermaid, and Jack ordered his usual whatever-was-on-tap.

Libby jotted their preferences down, biting her lip and glancing over at the entrance a couple of times.

"Everything okay, Libby?" Jack asked.

Libby looked startled. "Sure, Chief!"

Jack was smiling, but his gaze was serious, searching. "Yeah?"

Libby colored prettily, shot Jack a quick wary look. "Of course. We're just so busy!"

The pub was packed, no question. The Salty Dog always did a lively trade, but during tourist season it was hard to get a seat inside Pirate Cove's most popular watering hole. There were lots of unfamiliar faces scattered among the crowd of regulars smooshed into every available stretch of table space. A few glum-faced regulars were drinking at the bar and conversing quietly with Tom. Every PICO resident understood the tourist trade of the summer months was what kept the majority of the island businesses afloat, but that didn't mean they had to like the seasonal invasion.

Libby was summoned to another table, and she gave Jack and Ellery a bright, meaningless smile before moving quickly away.

"What was that about?" Ellery asked.

Jack shook his head. "I don't know. Something's up with her, though."

To be honest, Ellery was surprised at Jack's... what would you call it? Perspicacity? When it came to the feelings of a teenaged girl. But maybe he shouldn't have been. One reason Jack was such a good police chief was he paid close attention to everything that happened in "his" little burg. The other reason he was a good police chief was he truly cared about the health and welfare of every one of his constituents, even the ones not old enough to vote.

"I think it might have to do with Felix," Ellery said.

Jack's formidable brows drew together. "What do you mean?"

"I think he's struggling with everything that happened last month. Dylan told me last night Felix has quit the Scallywags."

Felix was Libby's boyfriend and the son of Pirate Cove's former mayor, Cyrus Jones. His parents were in the middle of a scandalous divorce—among other things—and it was no secret that Philippa Jones was weighing moving away from Buck Island.

Jack nodded thoughtfully. "That's too bad. The last thing that kid needs is to cut himself off from his support system."

"He may not have a choice if he and Philippa move to the mainland."

"True."

"Anyway, he and Libby will both be going away to college in the fall. Maybe the problem will sort itself out."

"Maybe." Jack was not in the let-problems-sort-themselves-out business.

"How's your burglary investigation coming?"

Jack grimaced. "Early days. None of the stolen goods have shown up at any pawn shop on the island. Which is no surprise."

"The thieves would be pretty stupid to try and off-load their loot here."

"Most criminals aren't geniuses, despite what mystery authors would have us believe."

Ellery grinned. He agreed. "True. But think how boring it would be to read police reports before bed."

"Hey, it works for me." But Jack was grinning back at him.

They chatted about nothing in particular, and then Libby returned with their drinks and proceeded to take their food order. Clam cakes and shoestring fries for Ellery and the rib-eye steak "special" for Jack.

Ellery took a cautious sip of his blue martini. "What's happening in the Maples case?" he inquired. One of the biggest eye-openers for him had been how very slowly the wheels of justice ground. Not so in crime fiction.

"Not a lot," Jack replied. "Our perp is still pleading not guilty, still trying to insist it was all a big misunderstanding."

"How can murder be a misunderstanding?"

Jack shrugged.

The Fish and Chippies, the Salty Dog's house band, arrived, guitars and mandolins in hand. It looked to Ellery like they had added an accordion player since their last performance—a slender dark-haired woman carried a baby in a backsack and a heavy, old-fashioned accordion case. The musicians made their way through the crowd to the small stage and began pulling out instruments and setting up mic stands and speakers.

"How's the new script coming?" Jack interrupted his thoughts.

Ellery groaned, and Jack chuckled.

"It can't be that bad."

"Can't it?" Ellery asked darkly.

"The play was great. This will be great too."

"The play was 'great'"—Ellery made air quotes—"for all the wrong reasons."

"No." Jack seemed sincere, even serious. "I don't buy that. If people love something, then they love it. How can there be a wrong reason?"

"Did you ever hear the phrase 'guilty pleasure'?"

"Sure, but *Murder Mansion* hardly qualifies as a guilty pleasure."

"How about…everyone thought it was a comedy, but it wasn't?"

Jack laughed. "Come on, a lot of that was written tongue-in-cheek."

Ellery made a face. "Maybe. Not all of it, though."

"It just means you're funnier than you give yourself credit for."

Ellery groaned again.

He was saved from further embarrassment by Libby's arrival with their meals. Even the suspicious speed with which their dinner had appeared couldn't discourage him from tucking in. What was there not to love about salt, grease, and fat perfectly prepared? Or even *not* perfectly prepared?

Jack ordered another round and winked at Ellery.

Argh. That effortless—unconscious—charm of Jack's was part of the problem. It wasn't like Jack went out of his way to be attractive. If anything, he considered his good looks a liability. But he was very good-looking. The navy-blue uniform emphasized his lean, fit body. His green-blue eyes sparkled with intelligence and good humor. His sun-streaked brown hair, damp, as though he'd showered before leaving the police station, fell boyishly across his forehead. Just the simple scents of soap and aftershave gave Ellery a funny feeling in the pit of his stomach. That was probably hunger and nothing to do with Jack at all. That's what he told himself anyway.

Tom Tulley stopped by their table, absently dabbing at a few drops of moisture on the tabletop. "Well, well. How are my two favorite customers this evening?"

Jack's smile was sardonic. Ellery said, "You say that to all your customers."

"All my favorites," Tom agreed, with a twinkle in his eye. "How are you two for drinks?"

"We're good," Jack said.

"Everything else okay? How's the food?"

"Terrific," lied Jack. "How's business?"

"Can't complain," lied Tom.

The three of them shot the breeze for a few more moments before Tom excused himself.

The Fish and Chippies went through the tedious but necessary task of mic check.

"One, two. One, two," drawled the dark-haired accordion player. Fish, the lanky leader of the band, beamed at her. The two existing "chippies" glared at him and then glared at her.

There was a story for sure.

Ellery was about to share this thought with Jack, when Jack said very casually, "What do you think about going diving this Sunday?"

They had talked about Jack teaching Ellery to dive on their one and only date. The waters around Buck Island were supposed to be littered with the wrecks of pirate ships. Ellery had assumed the offer had vanished with Jack's interest in pursuing a romantic relationship.

It was very tempting to say yes, but common sense—or maybe self-preservation—asserted itself. Ellery said, "I wish. But I've been thinking I probably shouldn't take any more Sundays off until the fall. We're too busy right now. It's not fair to ask Nora to cover the bookshop all on her own."

Jack looked disconcerted and then disappointed. "Oh. Right."

And maybe—probably—it was a sort of petty, but Ellery was glad he had said no. Clearly, Jack assumed he would say yes. Clearly, Jack had been hesitant about asking Ellery in the first place, in case Ellery misinterpreted the invitation.

Not likely.

Ellery said lightly, "Besides, who knows how hungover I'll be after a night of dancing, drinking, and ghost-hunting."

Jack's brows drew together. "What? You're planning to attend the Marauder's Masquerade? You know it's invitation only, right?"

"Right." Ellery grinned, although he was a little taken aback at the severity of Jack's expression. Did Jack really think he would try to gatecrash the ball? "It looks like I rate." He fished out the small black envelope and handed it to Jack.

Jack took it without looking away from Ellery's face. "Do you know the Bloodworths?"

"Nope."

"I don't understand."

"Me neither. But I can't pass up the social event of the season." Ellery was still smiling, still joking, but his pleasure was fading a bit at Jack's clear disapproval. Why should Jack care if Ellery attended the Marauder's Masquerade?

Even though he'd handed the invitation to Jack, he was irked when Jack opened the envelope to frown over the card inside. Did he think Ellery was mistaken? Lying? Did he think Ellery had forged his invitation?

Without comment, Jack tucked the card in its envelope and handed the invitation back to Ellery.

"Am I free to go, Officer?" Ellery couldn't help the edge that crept into his voice. He wasn't imagining it; Jack was definitely not thrilled Ellery had been invited to the Bloodworths' party.

Jack heard the note of irritation and offered a brief smile. "Yep. Congratulations." His gaze lifted, eyes scanning the crowd milling behind Ellery. Almost like he was dismissing him? No. That couldn't be right.

Could it?

It was second nature for Jack to keep an eye on his surroundings at all times. Ellery got that, but this just felt off.

"Is there any reason I shouldn't go?"

Jack's bright gaze dropped to meet his own. He shook his head. "No, of course not. If fancy dress balls are your thing, you'll have a great time."

"I don't know if they're my thing. But the ghost hunt sounds fun, and it's not like my social calendar is exactly jam-packed these days."

In fairness, it was more jam-packed than it had been a few months ago. Every Monday he had a date with the Monday Night Scrabblers and, like it or not, he was pretty much a member of the Scallywags, Pirate's Cove amateur theater guild. Once or twice a month he popped in to see how the Silver Sleuths and other book clubs were faring. He had friends now—including Jack. He was not nearly as lonely as he had been when he'd first moved to the island.

Jack grimaced. "Right. No, you should go. You'll have a good time. You deserve a night out."

Well, at least Jack was making an effort, saying the right things.

The Fish and Chippies launched into a lively version of Pete Seeger's "Hard Times in the Mill."

Ellery ate in silence, listening to the band while surreptitiously keeping an eye on Jack. Their former easy comradery had evaporated like sea spray on the summer breeze.

When Jack showed no sign of breaking the silence, Ellery said, "I didn't make the connection until today, but the masquerade is being hosted by your burglary victims?"

"The Bloodworths, yeah."

"That's..."

Interesting?

Abruptly, Ellery couldn't think of anything else to say. He was baffled by Jack's reaction to his invitation to the Masquerade.

Jack finished his beer, glanced at Ellery's still full glass, considered, and then seemed to decide against.

The band finished their number, and the accordion player launched into a moody version of "My Jolly Sailor Bold." Her voice was velvety smooth and sonorous.

"There is nothing can console me, but my jolly sailor bold..."

Certainly poor little Maria Catalina Isabella Bloodworth would have agreed with that.

Ellery concentrated on his food. The clam cakes were tender on the inside, deliciously crispy and brown on the outside. What he liked best about the Salty Dog's cuisine was that they caught fish fresh from the cove itself. You could spot Tom down at the wharf, collecting his haul every Friday morning.

He took another sip of his martini and searched for some neutral topic. "I hear you're Mr. July."

He had to raise his voice to be heard over the crowd and the band. A few of the pub's patrons glanced their way.

Jack looked startled, then mildly uncomfortable, throwing a quick look at the tables around them. "Oh. Uh, yeah. I mean, it's for a good cause."

"Exactly."

Jack studied him. "Does that mean you're part of next year's calendar?"

"Mr. April," Ellery admitted.

"You'll be the most popular month of the year," Jack assured him. The compliment would have been nicer if Jack's mouth hadn't had that ironic curve.

"Sure."

Jack's expression changed. "Sure you will. You're gorgeous."

It was sincere, even slightly impatient, as though he thought Ellery was being falsely modest, and Ellery's face warmed uncomfortably.

"I wouldn't say that."

"I would," Jack said. He turned his attention back to the stage, leaving Ellery feeling more confused than ever.

It was kind of a relief when they finished their meals and Jack signaled for the bill.

As much as Ellery enjoyed spending time with Jack, the evening had taken an awkward turn, and he wasn't even sure why.

Jack paid the bill, brushing aside Ellery's offer to split it. "I invited you, remember?"

Yes, Ellery did remember. He wished he didn't suspect Jack regretted that invitation.

They edged their way to the door, pausing to say hellos and goodbyes at crowded tables as they went, before pushing out into the muggy July night.

The day had been warm, and the evening was slow to cool. The sea air was rife with the scent of the harbor and fried fish. The pub door swung shut, cutting off a rousing version of "Go Down You Red Roses."

"That new singer is great," Ellery was saying. He broke off at the sight of a short, stocky kid stretched out on the long wooden bench next to the doorway. The boy—he was maybe nineteen or twenty—gazed back at Ellery and Jack with bright, challenging eyes. His hair was spiky and dark, and he wore ripped jeans and a black T-shirt that read: *Whale oil beef hooked.*

Ellery didn't recognize him, but Jack did. Jack said, "What did you need, Ned?"

"Just waiting for Libby," Ned said shortly.

"Maybe there's a better place for that?"

"Is there some law against me waiting here?"

Jack smiled. "Could be. You want me to check?"

Ned's face tightened. He sat up. "No."

"I'm thinking if Libby wants to meet up, she'll let you know."

Ned pushed up from the bench, threw Jack a look of intense dislike, and strode away down the cobbled sidewalk.

"Who's that?" Ellery asked as the boy vanished into the shadows.

"Ned Shandy." Jack sighed. "Not a bad kid, but getting to be a pain in the ass for Tom."

For Tom? And for Jack. Clearly.

Did Libby have any say in the matter? But Ellery didn't voice that thought. The evening had been problematic enough. He was pleasantly surprised to find that Jack was apparently walking him to his car.

He said at random, "Do you think there will be more burglaries?"

"I'm sure there will." Then Jack made a sound of amusement. "Is that association of ideas at work?"

"I'm not sure I—" Ellery glanced at Jack's steely profile. "You mean you suspect Ned Shandy of burglarizing the Bloodworths?"

"He's on my list of suspects."

"Yikes. How long is your list of suspects?"

"Not that long. Like I said, he's not a bad kid, but unfortunately he doesn't seem to have any direction in life."

That was a problem. There was a genuine lack of opportunity for young people on the island. Most of them ended up moving away to the mainland.

"He's still pretty young. Nineteen? Twenty?"

"Twenty-three." Jack glanced at him. "In answer to your question, we had another burglary last night." Jack corrected, "Attempted burglary."

"You're kidding. I didn't hear anything about it."

"Not something I want to advertise. Last night they hit the Maples' house."

"The Maples' house? I didn't realize there was anything left to steal. I thought a distant cousin of Trevor's packed everything up and shipped it West."

"Your intelligence is better than our burglar's."

"How many houses have been hit?"

"Three attempts so far. Only two have been successful."

"I really do need to get that security system installed at Captain's Seat." Ellery was thinking aloud.

Jack said, "Yes. You really do. So far, though, our burglars seem to strike at night, which could mean they have day jobs. And, with the exception of the Maples' place, the focus has been on vacation homes. Vacation homes without surveillance cameras."

Which was most of the vacation homes on the island.

"Burglars," Ellery repeated. "So you do think more than one person is involved?"

"Too soon to say for sure. So far everything has been small and portable: jewelry, money, silver, small appliances. No safes have been broken into. Nothing larger than a small television has been stolen."

"Maybe they're just getting started," Ellery said.

"That's what I'm afraid of."

They turned the corner onto the narrow brick street where the Crow's Nest cuddled between the Toy Chest and Sandy Morita's art gallery. The tall retrofitted gas lamps cast triangles of golden light on the empty street.

They fell silent, their feet sounding hollowly on the cobblestones as they strolled in and out of the deep shade of the tall Victorian buildings. Most of the shops were closed now, the storefronts shuttered or illuminated only by the ghostly glow of emergency lights.

Pirate's Cove was probably the safest place Ellery had ever lived, but late at night there was something otherworldly about the village. Maybe it was the ever-present, even looming, shadow of the island's occasionally sinister history.

They finally reached the Crow's Nest.

"I'll just pop next door and grab Watson," Ellery said. "Thanks for dinner, Jack."

"You're very welcome." Jack seemed to hesitate.

It had been such a weird night. First the surprise invitation from Jack, then Jack seeming to close down mid-dinner, and now this awkward moment of delay.

What the heck, Ellery thought, and he reached for Jack, hands landing on Jack's wide shoulders, drawing him forward till their mouths touched.

Jack's mouth was cool and firm, tasting of beer and steak spice, tasting of Jack.

Ellery tried to deepen the kiss.

Jack remained motionless, lips parting, then pressing closed. He covered Ellery's hands with his own, holding them warmly—and moving Ellery back.

It wasn't ungentle, but it was a definite no.

Thanks, but no thanks.

Which…hurt.

Gentle or not, the rejection hurt and embarrassed Ellery. Not that it wasn't his own fault. Jack had made it abundantly clear he did not want anything more than friendship. But after all, it was just a kiss. Jack had kissed *him* not so long ago. Ellery hadn't turned it into a federal case. Friends kissed each other sometimes.

Hopefully Jack did not see everything Ellery was feeling, but being observant and attentive to details, he probably did.

"Drive safe," Jack said.

"You too," Ellery said, which made no sense given that Jack lived in Pirate's Cove and was in walking distance of home.

Aggravated with himself as well as Jack, Ellery turned and sprinted up the stairs to Sandy Morita's apartment above the gallery next door.

When he reached the top landing, he couldn't resist glancing down.

The sidewalk below was empty.

CHAPTER FOUR

Ellery didn't realize he was talking to himself on the drive home until Watson, curled on the seat beside him, suddenly moaned as though he couldn't take it anymore.

Ellery gave a half laugh. "Sorry, buddy." He spared the pup a quick look. He could just make out the whites of Watson's eyes in the light from the dashboard.

"It's my own fault. I need to not..."

But there he ran out of ideas.

He really did like Jack a lot. He wanted to stay friends. The problem was his attraction to Jack made it difficult. But it wasn't fair to blame Jack for what Ellery was feeling. It wasn't Jack's fault Ellery had been more attracted to Jack than Jack had been to him. After all, it was a common problem for Jack.

He sighed, switched on the VW's CD player. Harry Styles singing "I'm So Lonely" came on.

"Uh, no. No way." Ellery punched the button for the next CD.

Clare Wyndham's ghostly voice wafted from the speakers. "Every Ending is a Chance."

Really? The universe—or at least his CD player—seemed to be trying to tell him something. His gaze moved briefly from the dark and mysterious road ahead to the countryside sliding past like scenes from a spooky music video. Twisted silhouettes and gleaming eyes. A razor-sharp scythe of moon that cast little light drifted aimlessly across the purple sky. Through the tangle of trees and hedges, a few random twinkles indicated where "summer folks" were in residence.

As the VW bounced over one of the inevitable potholes, Ellery did a double take. That was funny. It looked like lights were on at the Barby place.

The Barbys were good customers when they were on the island. They'd even attended a couple of book signings at the Crow's Nest. Mrs. Barby was partial to "anyone like Mary Higgins Clark except her daughter," and Mr. Barby liked military thrillers, "the more bloody, the better." Having made his money on Wall Street, Mr. Barby was always trying to give Ellery investment advice.

"No oil, Ellery. Don't invest in oil. It's a slippery slope, my boy. Take it from me." He was not being ironic.

The thing was, Ellery was pretty sure the Barbys were off-island for July. Mrs. Barby had been burbling about the joys of spending July in the Bahamas the last time they'd spoken.

He'd have put the blazing lights down to a timer, except he'd never before noticed lights on at the Barbys' when they weren't home.

He couldn't help remembering his conversation with Jack about the rash of vacation-homes burglaries. It would be kind of a coincidence to blunder onto a burglary in progress twenty minutes later. But coincidences *did* happen.

Even so…

He pulled a quick U-ie and doubled back toward the Barbys. Watson stuck his nose in the air and began sniffing as though smelling trouble.

"It won't hurt to take a quick look."

Ellery parked behind a wall of trees and cut the engine. Watson began to try and wriggle out of his car harness.

Ellery opened his car door and climbed out into the humid night air. He said firmly, "No. You're staying here. I won't be long. I'm sure it's nothing."

Watson had plenty to say about that, and it was all very loud. *If you're sure it's nothing, why are we parked down here? Why are you leaving ME?* seemed to be the gist of it.

Ellery swore inwardly but kept walking. A few yards on, the pup's voice had faded to annoying insect level. Which, given the symphony of crickets surrounding him, was still pretty loud.

He debated phoning Jack, but just because the Barbys had intended to summer in the Bahamas didn't mean they hadn't had a change of plans. Maybe they had returned home early. He was probably being paranoid. No need to make a fool of himself. He would just take a quick look and make sure everything was kosher. And if everything *wasn't* kosher, he could phone Jack then.

Halfway up the paved drive, he heard an engine and dived into the tall privet hedge. Just in time. A white van hurtled over the crest of the hill and roared down the road past him. Ellery peered at the windows but was unable to make out the figure hunched behind the wheel. The license plate was smeared over with mud.

For a second or two he crouched there, heart thumping, as the red taillights vanished down the highway. He pushed out of the flowering branches and continued up the hill, sticking to the deep shade till he reached the top of the drive.

Every light in the house appeared to be on. So…a good sign? Maybe not.

The house had started life as a single-story beach bungalow. The Barbys had made a number of home improvements, including a gazebo and, most notably, a front deck with a firepit. Ellery couldn't help noticing all the patio furniture had been put away for the season. Nor was there any sign of Skipper, the Barbys' wire fox terrier and four-legged alarm system. And, ominously, the teal-colored front door stood wide open.

Ellery crouched by the hedge, watching, but saw no sign of anyone.

After a minute or two, he sprinted to the corner of the raised deck and waited again for any sign that he had been discovered.

When the only sounds that met his ears were the crickets and night birds, he moved quietly along the deck, down the side of the house—staying low to avoid the brightly lit windows—and finally across the back of the house until he came to the big kitchen windows overlooking a putting green.

He was going to feel very silly if the Barbys were sitting out back, having a glass of wine in their gazebo.

But the Barbys were not sitting out back. There was no sign of anyone, inside or out.

Cautiously, Ellery raised his head over the sill and peered through the window.

The spacious kitchen featured black granite counters, an open-island setup, and gleaming stainless-steel appliances. A small fleet of wine bottles crowded every bit of space on the counter and island. One solitary wineglass sat out on the bench, with a tipple in it.

Either the Barbys were having one heck of a wine-tasting party, or their cellar was being liquidated. Ellery was pretty sure it was the latter.

The house appeared to be empty. Were the burglars making trips back and forth with their loot? That much wine wasn't going to be easy to safely transport. You couldn't leave dozens of wine bottles bouncing around the back of a van.

A door led from the kitchen into a huge living room. From Ellery's vantage point, he could see a large natural-stone fireplace, a humongous wall-mounted TV, and an elaborate stereo system with what looked to be surround sound.

Wouldn't burglars want that TV set and stereo system? But no, Jack had said the thieves only took small, easily portable objects. That TV was the size of a small sofa.

As Ellery considered, someone moved past the living-room doorway.

He ducked down, breathing fast.

Okay. Thank God he hadn't made the mistake of going inside. It seemed that not all the burglars had gone in the van.

He needed to phone Jack now.

Actually, he needed to have phoned Jack half an hour ago. But now was better than never.

Ellery found his phone, the screen lighting as he scrolled for Jack's number.

The *crunch* of footsteps on gravel reached his ears, and his heart sprang into alarmed tempo. Someone was coming.

He thrust his phone in his jeans pocket, dousing the light. How the heck many people were on the premises? This wasn't a gang; it was a freaking army.

He dived toward the path leading to the gazebo, wincing at the *crackle* of dead leaves underfoot. Once again he slipped into the shrubs—this time rose-bushes and less welcoming. He smothered a yelp as a thorny branch scraped across his cheek, just missing his eye. He prayed for the branches to stop moving.

The silence seemed to reverberate. He waited, trying to hear over the rush of blood in his ears. Maybe he'd... Maybe they'd...

His heart nearly stopped at the sharp whistle from behind him. He peered cautiously through the leaves and saw a shadowy figure at the head of the path.

Oh no.

Oh hell.

Had he been seen?

Was there any chance he *hadn't* been seen?

He began to push backward through the roses, trying to stay silent, trying not to move the shrubberies. Good luck with that, Natty Bumppo. The bushes were probably heaving like an ocean of leaves and thorns as he forced his way through.

He paused, trying to orient himself, trying to figure out where the others were in relation, listening tautly, every muscle strung tight, praying...

Nothing. Not a sound.

At least, not a sound not of his own making.

Even the crickets were hushed.

Cautiously, carefully, Ellery inched his head above the leaves, eyes straining the gloom.

Mistake.

Another of those piercing whistles split the night, and the figure at the head of the path pointed down the uneven trail.

He was being hunted.

CHAPTER FIVE

No point trying for stealth now. Ellery shoved through the rosebushes, protecting his bare hands and arms as much as he could, which wasn't much. He burst out into a small clearing. A large pond surrounded by reeds gleamed in the moonlight. On the far side of the pond was a tall, weathered old building with a steeply pointed roof.

It wasn't a barn, unless it was a barn for mountain goats. Was it a mini sawmill? He studied the double doors—one ajar—and a steep ramp leading inside and to another smaller set of doors beneath the eaves.

An icehouse. He remembered Nora talking about how back in the old days, harvesting and storing ice in these thick-walled structures had been a lucrative business. In the summer, the carefully preserved supply of ice was sold to the island's hotels and inns for the tourist trade.

None of the commercial icehouses still existed, but a few of the grand old homes still had the ruins of those structures on their grounds. The Barbys' bungalow was of recent, modern construction, so he must have crossed their property line. He searched the darkness for any sign of lights, any sign of another house, but saw nothing.

Ellery skirted the pond, hoping to reach the safety of the trees beyond, but a shrill whistle up ahead froze him in his tracks.

He was running out of options fast. He circled the building, and then, reluctantly, slipped inside. For a moment he stood there, panting, letting his eyes adjust to the pitchy darkness. It was tempting to close the door, but since he had no way to lock it, it wouldn't do much good. Whereas if he left the door open, his pursuers might figure he had chosen not to go inside.

Unless they were following his own line of reasoning.

If you could call his panicked thoughts reason.

Ellery felt the cold, dank breath of pond water. Moonlight spilled through the overhead vent only to be swallowed by the black, still pond a few inches from the wooden walkway. There was virtually no illumination beyond that single ray of light.

Hand outstretched, he stepped cautiously along the wooden planks, leaning against the wall, until something invisible in the dark scuttled over his face. He swallowed a yell and then listened intently.

Were those footsteps? He held motionless. Tried not to breathe.

Yes. Footsteps moving along the side of the building.

Were they armed? Would they come inside and shoot him? No. No, surely not. Why would they? But why were they chasing him? Why didn't they flee?

Why hadn't he phoned Jack when he had the chance?

Why hadn't he phoned Jack from the safety of his car?

Because he hadn't wanted to look foolish.

He pressed his ear to the rough wooden plank.

Were those whispers? Yes. A whispered discussion.

He couldn't make out the words, but the tone indicated disagreement.

The whispering stopped, and the silence that followed was truly terrifying.

What now? Was there someplace he could—

The open door to the icehouse slammed shut with such force, a few slats fell off the roof and splashed into the pond nearby.

Ellery stood rooted in place as footsteps pounded down the wooden walkway and faded into the night.

Silence descended. An absolute and utter silence but for the dismal gurgling of the pond in the center of the building.

Ellery turned on his phone's flashlight and moved the beam slowly around the building. He could see that the horseshoe-shaped walkway where he stood was missing several planks. He could see the black pool of dank water slurping at the soggy ground a few feet from the walkway. He held the light up and saw bird nests, monster spiderwebs, and a rusted block and tackle.

Carefully, he made his way back to the double doors and pushed against them. The doors bowed but stayed shut.

He had seen no lock, so he pushed again.

Again, the doors held.

Somehow they were blocked or had been wedged shut, and he was effectively locked in.

Ten fraught minutes passed as Ellery tried to find another way out. There wasn't one, and a couple of slips on the slimy planks convinced him fumbling around in the dark was a good way to break his neck. He considered the ladder leading to the top level, but it was missing too many rungs.

However little he liked it, the only way out was through the double doors. Okay. Given that the entire building looked ready to collapse any moment, the doors couldn't be that much of a challenge. Right?

Wrong.

Ellery spent several more minutes tugging and kicking uselessly at splintering slats, but the structure was sturdier than it appeared. Finally, in frustration, he tried body-slamming the opening between the two doors. *Yowch.* He was forced to accept that his shoulder would break before that door gave an inch.

Now what?

Ellery shivered. Despite the warm July night, it was cold in the icehouse. Not as cold as it would have been stacked with blocks of ice, but colder than was comfortable. Part of the chill, though, was simply nerves.

Nerves over what had been. Nerves over what was to come. Because there really was only one move left to him.

He checked his phone screen, relieved to see a signal—until he noticed the red battery sign.

10%.

His fingers shook as he typed the numbers.

Two very long rings before Jack answered.

"Let me guess. Car trouble?" Jack sounded resigned.

"Wellllll, no," Ellery admitted.

"No?"

"Kind of a long story, but—"

"Give me the CliffsNotes," Jack was terse. God. Did he imagine Ellery was coming up with lame excuses to contact him?

"I'm locked in the old icehouse behind the Barby property."

The resounding silence on Jack's end stretched.

Ellery felt a flash of alarm. Had the call dropped? "Jack? Are you there?"

Jack said slowly, doubtfully, "Did you say you're—"

"I did, yeah." He hated that his voice wobbled a little.

He heard what sounded like a sharp inhale. "Are you hurt? Have you been injured?"

"No. No, I'm okay. Just cold. I can explain everything, if you could just—"

"Can you?"

Ouch. That was Chief Carson talking. An unamused Chief Carson. Not that there was much amusement value in the situation.

"I can try. Listen, my phone is dying. Could you please send someone to unlock th-this door?" His teeth were starting to chatter with that mixture of cold and nerves.

"Let me think about it."

"Hey," Ellery protested. "This isn't funny."

"You got that right." It sounded like Jack was moving around, his terse voice rising and falling as he did whatever it was he was doing. Hopefully he was getting dressed. Although, come to think of it, maybe it would be better if he sent someone like Officer Martin to the rescue.

"Please, Jack."

Jack said gruffly, "I'm coming. Stay put." He disconnected.

Stay put? Like he had any choice?

It seemed like he waited a lifetime in that frigid black silence, but it was probably no more than forty-five minutes before Ellery heard the *snap-crunch* of boots on stone. The doors wobbled beneath some assault, there was a sound of a board falling away, and the double doors opened with a rusty screech of protest. Moonlight poured in.

Jack's figure stood silhouetted in the wide doorway.

"Ellery?"

"Right here." Ellery practically leaped off the walkway and through the door.

"You okay?"

"Y-y-yes."

"Here." Jack was still terse as he pushed a slick folded square of silver into Ellery's hands.

The silver square turned out to be a thermal blanket, which Ellery shook the folds out of and wrapped around himself like a shawl. "I r-r-ran into your b-b-burglars."

"Yeah, I know."

"You do?"

"I had a quick look around. It looks like they emptied the wine cellar, among other things."

It took a couple of moments for that to fully register. Ellery stared at Jack's moonlit profile.

"How long have you been here?"

Jack said coolly, "About fifteen minutes."

"Fifteen… You've been here fifteen minutes?"

"That's right." Ellery was trying to tell himself it wasn't actually the way it sounded, when Jack erased all doubt and added, "I didn't think it would hurt you to spend a little longer on ice."

Ellery gaped at him. "You— Are you kidding me? You deliberately left me in there?"

"I was hoping you'd have enough time to consider why playing amateur sleuth is a really bad idea. I sure as hell did."

Until then, Ellery hadn't understood how angry Jack truly was.

And that made two of them because the realization that Jack had left him sitting in that black hole for an extra quarter of an hour made Ellery so mad, he could barely control his voice. His hand shook as he pointed to the structure behind them.

"Let me make sure I understand. *You left me freezing in there to teach me a lesson*?"

"I figured you'd prefer that to spending the night in a jail cell."

"*S-s-spending a night in jail?* For what?"

Jack was unmoved by Ellery's shout of protest. "We can start with Failure to Report a Crime and go on from there."

"Failure to— I didn't have time to report anything. You—"

"Nonsense," said Jack, only he didn't say *nonsense*, and his voice was now as loud as Ellery's. "You could have called this in when you first parked down by the highway. Clearly, you thought something was up. You could have called this in at any point when you hiked up the drive to the house. You chose not to, and you're lucky you're not finishing this evening up *dead*. You don't have any idea what weapons the perpetrator may have had. You have no idea what their state of mind was."

"I thought they'd left," Ellery argued. "I saw a white van leave, and I thought they were gone."

It was doubtful Jack heard him. He was too busy yelling, "You don't like the idea of spending a few hours in an icehouse? Well, I don't like the idea of you spending the rest of your life in a morgue."

"I wouldn't be spending my *life* in the morgue," Ellery shot back, which was a good indicator of how quickly the conversation was devolving.

"How you could do something so reckless, so idiotic—"

"I saw lights on and wondered if everything was okay. I didn't *know*. I didn't instantly *assume* someone was burgling the Barbys."

"Really? Because we'd been talking about that very thing not twenty minutes before."

"Which is why it seemed like too much of a coincidence."

Words seemed to fail Jack.

"What if I'd called you and it turned out their lights were on a timer? Or they had a house guest? Or the housekeeper left the lights on last time she was here? Or...I don't know! People in Pirate's Cove check on each other all the time. This is the isle of nosy neighbors. Why is my stopping to make sure everything is okay any different?"

"Because I know you," Jack said, and his voice was aggravatingly superior. "I know you thought you would do a little snooping—"

"You're so wrong."

"Am I?"

"Yes."

Although... Granted, it had started out exactly as Ellery said. But then, yes, he had let his curiosity get the better of him. It wasn't entirely curiosity, though. He hadn't wanted to call Jack and then turn out to be wrong.

Except he hadn't had to call Jack; he could have called the police station and got whoever was handling emergency calls that night.

He had made a judgment call that, yeah, turned out to be lacking in judgment. And if Jack hadn't been such a jerk as to leave him freezing his butt off in that icehouse, he'd have apologized by now instead of digging his heels in.

"Having contaminated my crime scene, tell me you at least got the license plate number of the van you saw leaving the scene."

Ellery didn't bother arguing about crime scene contamination. For all he knew, he *had* contaminated the outside perimeter. He could easily have trampled over footprints.

"The license plate was smeared with something dark. Mud, I think. I couldn't read it."

"Great."

Stung, Ellery said, "It was a battered white Ford van. An older model."

"That's pretty much every delivery van on the island."

"No signs or decals."

"Did you get a look at the driver?"

Ellery shook his head. "No. I didn't see anyone's face. There were at least three of them. The driver of the van and the two who chased me into the icehouse."

Jack's face got tight again. He let out a long careful breath like someone defusing a bomb. But he said quite mildly, "Anything else you can remember that might be helpful? Did you hear them speak? Did you hear them call each other by name?"

"They whistled to alert each other. I didn't hear them speak. I did hear them whispering outside the icehouse, but I couldn't make out any words. I wouldn't be able to identify their voices."

"Male or female? Could you tell?"

"No. Whispers are sexless."

Jack nodded, though not in acknowledgment or approval, and jotted down some quick notes in the small leather notebook he always carried.

Ellery watched him. "I'm thinking Ned Shandy has an alibi."

"Oh? Is that what you're thinking?"

Ellery's temper rose again. "Are we done here?"

"Yes." Jack regarded him for a moment, seemed to consider and then discard what he was about to say. "You can go."

Ellery turned and went without another word.

CHAPTER SIX

*H*ouse of Blood.

That's what they called Bloodworth Manor back in the seventeenth century. And in the crimson rays of the setting sun, the house lived up to that reputation. It was a two-story, rectangular, redbrick building with white-stone facings, four chimneys, and a multitude of tall, narrow, paired windows and scarlet, heavily molded double doors.

It was no Captain's Seat. Clearly, Thomas Bloodworth had been trying to recapture some of the homey feel of the family estate in Dorset.

Ellery had parked at the bottom of the regal drive and was hiking past a very long line of awkwardly parked cars and golf carts toward the house. He was not alone. Several other couples in Georgian, Regency, and Fantasy-pirate finery made the climb with him, all of them shuffling ungracefully to the side as the occasional limo prowled soundlessly up behind them.

It was actually the same limo and the same driver. Sam Cuddlefish owned the island's only taxi service. Sam had one limousine, which he insisted on driving despite the fact that he was now in his late eighties. Sam and the limo were getting a workout that evening as Buck Island's elite tried to stagger their entrances around each other.

The regular folks drove themselves, parked on the drive, and hiked up to the mansion.

As Ellery topped the crest of the drive, he saw two reporters from the *Scuttlebutt Weekly* snapping photos of people making their grand entrances.

With Sam's help, an elderly couple in full costume exited the limo, paused for their photos to be taken, and swept their way down the red carpet and into the mansion.

It wasn't up to Hollywood premiere standards, but it was impressively close. A small contingent of brocade and wig-clad footmen waited out front with trays of champagne and scented misters to refresh the wilted guests making the trek on foot.

"Avast, me heartie," Dylan's voice reached Ellery's ears, and he glanced around.

"Hey."

Dylan looked fantastic in a gold-trimmed, navy-blue pirate vest. He wore a wide gold sash around his narrow waist and black pantaloons. He even had a stuffed green parrot attached to his shoulder.

"You. Look. *Mahvellous*," Ellery said. "Love the bird."

Dylan hammed, "Bird? You say you love my bird? Is that what you say?"

"Gene Wilder, *Start the Revolution Without Me.*"

Dylan pointed at him. "Correct. Speaking of looking marvelous. Somebody should paint you in that outfit."

"This waistcoat is so tight, I'm not sure Nora didn't." No lie. He was afraid he was going to pop that row of little gold buttons every time he exhaled.

"Eat your heart out, Chief Carson," Dylan murmured.

Ellery threw him a quick look of alarm. "Jack? Jack isn't going to be at this thing, is he?"

"Pirate Cove's Chief of Police? Of course. If Chief Carson doesn't qualify as a VIP, I don't know who does. He's here every year."

Ellery scowled. He hadn't seen or spoken to Jack since Wednesday night, and he wasn't in a hurry for that to change.

Dylan had already heard the whole story of Jack and Ellery's run-in. Like Nora, he had tried to offer a more...mollifying view of events. He said again, "Carson can be abrasive, but I really do think he was scared at the idea of what might have happened to you."

"I know," Ellery said. Meaning he knew that was what Dylan thought, not that he agreed with him. From the first, Dylan had been of the opinion that Jack had reacted badly because he had feelings for Ellery. Ellery thought Jack had reacted out of what

Great-great-great-aunt Eudora would have called an "excess of spleen," and that Dylan was a lot more romantic than he'd suspected.

Okay, he was honest enough to admit, at least privately, that he could have been smarter in his handling of the situation at the Barbys'. He knew things could have ended badly for him. He could even believe that part of the reason Jack had been such an ass was because of his experience as a detective. Jack knew all about unexpected violence and tragic outcomes. But leaving his supposed "friend" sitting there in that spider-invested wreck, listening to the icy slurp of water and things scuttling in the darkness? Ellery was still angry.

Anyway, he was glad he had warning that he was liable to run into Jack—although it added to his irritation that Jack had not mentioned he was attending the Marauder's Masquerade when Ellery had shown him his invitation. Had he been afraid Ellery might ask to be his date? Who the heck knew with Jack?

What Ellery did know was he was tired of wondering about what Jack might be thinking.

In fact, he was tired of the very idea of Jack.

Ellery and Dylan paused for pics, gave their names to the photographers, accepted glasses of champagne, and followed the stream of guests up the red-carpeted steps lined with fairy lights and through the doorway beneath a lintel carved with schooners and sea monsters.

They entered a marble great hall dominated by a gigantic gold-framed portrait of a handsome seventeenth-century nobleman standing on a cliff, spyglass in hand. The man wore a long black cloak, and his tumbled pale locks blew in the wind from beneath a large-brimmed, plumed hat. His silvery-gray eyes seemed to stare down the centuries at them.

"Is that Tom Blood?" Ellery asked Dylan.

"That's the man," Dylan said. "Or possibly the legend. For all we know, he was three inches shorter and bow-legged."

"He was definitely shorter," Ellery said. "That portrait is about eleven feet tall."

"Good point."

According to *Pirates of New England*, Captain Blood had cut a pretty romantic figure, and the man in the portrait certainly looked heroic, but everything was relative.

They followed the crowd through a couple of marble columns, and Ellery had a quick impression of a huge room filled with candles and flowers and sparkling chandeliers and gold-framed paintings. Positioned between long mirrors, a string quartet were playing Schubert.

"It's like a scene from *Forever Amber*, isn't it?" Dylan said with satisfaction. They shared a love for corny vintage historical dramas, and Ellery grinned in agreement.

There were enough gowns and elaborate wigs and frock coats and breeches for three more *Pirates of the Caribbean* sequels. They couldn't all be provided by the Scallywags, so did that mean the citizens of Pirate's Cove kept a spare wardrobe of pirate garb?

He amused himself speculating about the secret lives of Pirate's Cove residents.

Most guests were sporting laser-cut Venetian-style masks, though some went in for traditional papier-mâché trimmed with braid or jewels or beads. One or two gentlemen, who had been likely dragged against their will, wore the squarish and more concealing Bauta-style masks that offered actual disguise, but mostly it wasn't hard to tell who was who.

And it did appear to be true that just about everyone who was anyone in Pirate's Cove was in attendance.

The crowd seemed to have narrowed to a receiving line. A tall woman stood at the head. She could have been any age between fifty and seventy. She was very thin but elegant in a silver satin and brocade gown trimmed with pearls and sequins and yards of foamy lace. Her platinum hair was swept up in elaborate knots of sparkling jewels and ribbon. Her mask was hardly more than a wisp of silvery lace and probably wasn't intended to be more than ornamental. The resemblance to the portrait in the great hall was striking.

"The Pirate's Granddaughter," Dylan murmured. "That's husband Number 2 with her."

Until Dylan pointed him out, Ellery hadn't even noticed Marguerite's companion. He was equally gorgeously clothed, in his case in blue velvet. He was shorter, dark-haired, blue-eyed. Definitely younger—

perhaps forty—and handsome, but starting to blur at the edges. He held one of those *Medico della Peste* masks with the long hollow beak and round eyes.

The queue moved forward, and Ellery found himself shaking the "Pirate's Granddaughter's" silver-tipped, perfectly manicured hand. From behind her mask, her cool, gray eyes met his.

"Ellery Page," Ellery introduced himself. "Thank you for inviting me, Mrs. Bloodworth-Ainsley."

Marguerite regarded him with an odd intensity and then offered a dazzling smile. "Julian's friend. Of course. We're so happy you could join us, Ellery." She glanced at her companion, who was joking with someone. She didn't speak, but he reacted as if she'd nudged him in the ribs.

He blinked from Marguerite to Ellery. "Yes, my angel? What's that?"

"Brett, this is Julian's friend, Ellery." Marguerite's voice was a smooth contralto.

"Nice to meet you, Ellery," Brett said automatically, shaking hands. His blue eyes had a slightly glassy look. That could have been too many drinks or too many introductions. He added vaguely, "Oh, right. Julian's friend."

Who the heck was Julian? And where did they get the notion Ellery and Julian were friends?

Was there a polite way to ask? Ellery had no idea and, in any case, there was no time. He had to admire the smooth way he was moved down the receiving line and handed off to a heavyset iron-haired man who introduced himself as Locke Lombard.

Ellery chatted briefly with Locke, who he knew owned the *Legacy*, a 213-foot yacht usually anchored in the harbor at Pirate's Cove. Locke introduced Ellery to several more people, all of whom fell in the category of summer folk and were strangers to him. Most professed amazement that there was a bookstore on the island.

At last Ellery escaped and was free to wander and investigate the really sumptuous spread of hors d'oeuvres, which included a variety of caviars, country pâté toasts, and pop-up oysters. There had not been time for lunch that day, and he was enjoying sampling everything until he spotted Philippa Jones, the soon-to-be ex-wife of Pirate Cove's former mayor, and made a quick about-face. He knew firsthand that Philippa held him to blame for all her family's misfortunes.

Funny how in most cozy mysteries, no one seemed to hold a grudge against the sleuth. Not so in real life. Which didn't feel quite fair. It wasn't like Ellery had ever set out to bring anyone to justice. Mostly his sleuthing had been forced upon him by outside circumstances. Regardless of what Jack thought.

In fact, Jack *was* one of those outside circumstances.

Anyway, Ellery's sharp turn brought him face-to-face with the editor and owner of the *Scuttlebutt Weekly*, Sue Lewis. She wasn't much older than him, petite, and pretty in a bronze satin gown with gold embroidery. Sue had not bothered trying to arrange her long, straight blonde hair in anything resembling historical accuracy, but she did wear a bronze satin mask.

"Hi, Sue," Ellery said.

Sue was no fonder of Ellery than Philippa, though with less reason (whether she knew it or not), and she smiled with narrowed eyes.

"Look who's here. The notorious Ellery Page."

"Notorious?" Ellery murmured. "That seems a bit much."

"If the pirate boots fit," Sue said.

They didn't actually, and Ellery was seriously beginning to regret letting Nora and Dylan pressure him into wearing them.

"Are you having a nice time?" Ellery asked. He really hated confrontation.

Unfortunately, Sue really loved it.

Her lips curled into a nasty smile. "Oh please. You don't fool me with that boy-next-door act."

"Now you know why I gave up acting." Ellery smiled too, and slipped past her.

He bumped literally into Dylan, who had stepped into an alcove to adjust his parrot.

"There you are," Dylan said. "I don't know about you, but I need a real drink."

"I don't think there's anything but champagne."

"The bar's on the terrace out back." Dylan hooked a thumb over his shoulder and knocked his parrot loose again. He swore.

"Here." Ellery did his best to fasten the drunkenly swaying parrot to the shoulder of Dylan's vest.

They headed through the crowded main room and out through one of the open Palladian doors leading onto the terrace. The air was cooler outside and smelled of freshly mown grass and night-blooming flowers.

The flagstone terrace was as large as the grand and formal room they just left. Tiny white lights were wound around giant urns and strung along the surrounding walls. People sat at small wooden tables, listening to the Fish and Chippies playing "Drunken Sailor." A few couples were trying to dance.

"It's like a different party out here," Ellery said.

"*Exactly.*" Dylan led the way to the bar on the other end of the terrace.

The line moved quickly, they got their drinks—you had to love a hosted bar—and moved away. Dylan was instantly waylaid by a woman hoping to audition for the Scallywags, and Ellery moved tactfully out of earshot.

There were no empty chairs at the tables, but he found a nice stretch of wall between the Palladian doors to lean against.

He was watching the band and the dancers when he noticed he was not alone.

A few feet away, a tall man was smiling at him. It was hard to be sure in the skittish light, but he seemed to be wearing black Gothic Death Pants, a doublet of indeterminate color, and a black mask that emphasized glittering light eyes.

"Hi," Ellery said.

That seemed to be all the invitation needed. The man joined him, smiling broadly in the gloom.

"Hello." He offered his hand. "I'm Julian Blood-worth."

"*Oh*. Hey," Ellery said. "Very nice to meet you."

"And you, of course, are Ellery Page."

"I am," Ellery admitted. "Thank you for the invite." They continued to smile at each other.

"Movie star, playwright, and amateur sleuth."

"Mostly humble bookseller," Ellery said, and Julian laughed as though Ellery had said something brilliantly funny.

"You're way too modest."

"Not really."

"I have to tell you, I love the Crow's Nest. When we were here in February, I was there every week buying books."

"Were you?" Ellery didn't remember Julian, but he'd been pretty preoccupied the first weeks he'd moved to Pirate's Cove. Also, still recovering from the breakup with Todd, he had been determinedly disinterested in meeting anyone new. A man as attractive as Julian would have had the reverse effect on him. "Thanks for supporting the shop."

"And I've seen *all* your movies a million times."

"It's actually the same movie over and over again," Ellery felt compelled to point out.

Again, Julian gave one of those shouts of laughter. "I'm so glad you decided to accept our invitation. I've been dying to meet you forever. I couldn't think of a way."

Ellery tilted his head, studying Julian. "You could always have come up and introduced yourself."

Julian made a face. He sounded almost nervous as he admitted, "I was afraid you'd think I was a stalker."

"Really? Are you a stalker?"

Julian laughed again. Said cheerfully, "You'll soon find out!"

They chatted some more about books and movies. By then both the band and the crowd were getting louder and livelier.

Julian said, "You want to go inside and find a corner where we can hear ourselves?"

"Sure," Ellery said.

They stepped inside the crowded room, and Julian slipped a companionable arm through Ellery's.

The violins were playing delicate counterpoint to a cello and viola.

"Where did you ever find a string quartet in Pirate's Cove?" Ellery asked. He knew Dylan was always on the hunt for musicians for the theater.

Julian seemed amused. "A family friend plays for the New York Symphony. She put this ensemble together for us."

"Wow, that's amazing."

"Yes. We're very grateful."

Julian was his own age or perhaps slightly younger. In the shimmering light from the chandeliers, Ellery could see that Julian's wavy hair was white-blond and his eyes were the same striking gray as his mother's. He was an attractive guy, no question.

"There won't be anyone in the..." Julian was saying.

Ellery missed the rest of it because they came face-to-face—well, actually, face-to-back—with Jack.

CHAPTER SEVEN

Ellery had been laying bets with himself that Jack would not deign to dress up for the ball, but he'd been wrong about that. Jack was in costume. Subdued costume, but definitely costume. He wore trim fawn breeches, a nicely fitted dark-brown frock coat, a brown tricorn, and brown pirate boots.

It didn't matter. In costume or out, from front or behind, he'd recognize Jack, and Ellery was very glad he'd had a heads-up about Jack being present because running into him unprepared would have been a jolt.

If they had still been on friendly terms, Ellery would have whistled—those fawn breeches did wonderful things for Jack's muscular thighs and long legs—but the situation being what it was, he settled for a quiet, "Ahoy there."

Jack glanced his way, did a double take. "Ahoy." He smiled, his teeth very white against his sober black mask. "Wow. You look…" His blue-green gaze flicked to Julian, took in the younger man's possessive grip of Ellery's arm, and something infinitesimal changed in his expression. He said politely, "How are you, Julian?"

"Hi, Chief." Julian was beaming. "I'm great now that the guest of honor has arrived."

Ellery blinked. *Guest of honor* was a little over-the-top, but Julian seemed to be a very enthusiastic person.

"Guest of honor?" Jack murmured. "I didn't realize you two knew each other."

"There's so much you don't realize," Ellery said. It was kind of silly, but satisfying in the moment. Between the icehouse and the rebuffed kiss, he was struggling with his feelings for Jack.

Jack's eyes narrowed. His smile was much cooler this time. "I see. Well, enjoy your evening, boys." He raised his barely touched champagne glass in salute, and moved away.

Boys. Ellery had to curb his irritation. Jack was thirty-eight, not sixty-eight. He muttered, "Funny. Even in pirate's clothing he looks like a cop."

"Like an exciseman," Julian joked. He added, "I used to have such a thing for him."

"You're kidding." Julian seemed prone to crushes. It was endearing, though he did seem young for his age. Assuming he was as old as Ellery was guessing. *Hopefully*, he was as old as Ellery was guessing.

"No." Julian grinned at whatever he thought he read in Ellery's expression. "I know. But there's something about that mix of hard-ass law enforcement and twinkly eyes."

"Twinkly eyes?" Ellery had never thought Jack's eyes particularly twinkly. They did crinkle at the corners when he smiled, that was true. And there was that crease in his cheek when he grinned. Not quite a dimple, but close. He'd give Julian that.

Unnervingly, Julian seemed to read his mind. "Yeah. And that grin. That boyish grin like he's sharing a private joke with you. That used to get me right here." Julian flattened his fist against his chest.

"Hm." Ellery was afraid to ask, but he felt compelled. "Did you two have a…a…?"

"Me and Police Chief Carson?" Julian laughed. "No way. He's straighter than a…a…"

Funny how hard-ass, twinkly eyed Jack could drive normally articulate men to incoherence.

"Yardarm?" Ellery suggested. "Ramrod? The red-hot poker jammed up his—"

Julian laughed, squeezed his arm affectionately. "You don't have to be jealous of Chief Carson. I got over that a long time ago." He glanced back at the terrace. "I didn't think. Did you want to dance?"

Ellery grimaced. "Not really."

Julian looked disappointed. "No?"

"I hate to admit it, but these boots are killing my feet."

Julian ogled Ellery's knee-high, black leather corsair boots.

"Those boots are seriously sexy. But maybe you should take them off. You have to save your feet for the ghost hunt. It's the best part of the night."

"If I take them off, I'll never get them on again."

Julian chuckled. He was a guy who laughed a lot. That was nice, right? Ellery was typically light-hearted himself.

Speaking of laughing a lot. A few feet away, Brett Ainsley was half-seated on a Louis XV Rococo giltwood console with a woman precariously balanced on his lap. They were both laughing loudly, so loudly that their voices carried over the music and the other guests. Ellery expected to see the console tip over any moment.

"Who's that?" Ellery asked.

"That's Brett," Julian said darkly. "My mother's so-called husband."

So-called husband? Ouch. No love lost there. Ellery was every bit as fond of his stepdad as he'd been of his father, but then George wasn't a drunken, womanizing lout. It wouldn't be easy watching your stepfather be so disrespectful to your mother.

"I meant the lady with him."

Julian muttered, "That's no lady; that's Klementina Harwood."

"Ah," said Ellery. He had no clue who that was. In fact, it was amazing to him that these Buck Island "elite" were largely unknown to him. Maybe because they were only on the island three months out of the year?

Ms. Harwood seemed to be channeling Elizabethan courtesan. She wore red velvet and pearls—more pearls than red velvet—which she swung in a little loop like a stripper preparing to saunter onstage. Her ridiculously ornate black wig was starting to slip as Brett nuzzled behind her ear. She shrieked with laughter and cried, "You're so *bad*."

"Come on," Julian muttered. "Let's go find someplace we can talk."

Ellery was in favor of that, but it was kind of like trying to swim against the current. Every few steps they were stopped by someone wanting to talk—usually with Julian—which meant Julian had to introduce Ellery, and then Ellery had to explain who he was and how it was no one had ever heard of him. Did *none* of these people read or attend the local theater or even subscribe to the *Scuttlebutt Weekly*?

The tall and stately eighteenth-century grandfather clock chimed the hours as they had more glasses of champagne, more hors d'oeuvres, more increasingly pointless conversations as their fellow guests became more and more inebriated, and eventually they ran into the lady of the manor.

Julian beamed. "Ellery, have you met my mother, Marguerite Bloodworth-Ainsley?"

"Yes, darling. We met earlier." Marguerite was smiling at Ellery. "Are you having a nice time, Ellery?"

"I'm having a great time," Ellery said truthfully. "It's a great party."

"I'm so glad. You own the bookstore in town, don't you?"

"Yes. The Crow's Nest."

"I used to go there when I was a girl. Your aunt was such an interesting woman. I remember the shop had all those wonderful old paintings of the sea."

"They're still there. Sadly, I never got to meet my Great-great-great-aunt Eudora."

"She was an original." Marguerite smiled again. "I wish I had more time to read. There's nothing more comforting than curling up with a good whodunit in front of the fire. Julian tells me you've done wonders to restore the shop."

"We're getting there," Ellery said.

"I'm sure you are. And, of course, you're the author of last month's wonderful play."

Ellery nearly choked on his champagne. He caught Marguerite's cool, silvery gaze, and though she never batted an eyelash, he felt as though she'd winked at him. As though she understood his feelings entirely, and both sympathized and was amused.

He liked her.

He hadn't expected to. She wasn't instantly likeable, but yes, he did like her. And he liked Julian.

It had been a long time since anyone had made him feel so attractive, so appreciated.

In fact, Julian was saying, "We never laughed so hard as we did driving home from that play. It was terrific."

Ellery smiled feebly.

Marguerite started to speak, but they were interrupted by a loud crash, the distinct sound of a slap, and then a sharp, furious scream.

The music cut off as abruptly as if someone had yanked the plug. There were gasps and shocked murmurs, and the crowd seemed to draw back like wilting petals from acid—or in this case, Brett Ainsley and Klementina Harwood.

The long rope of pearls Klementina had been swinging playfully had broken, and the pearls were bouncing and rolling across the marble floor in a sudden downpour.

"It was an *accident*, you bastard," she cried. Black eyeliner mingled with tears on her face. There was a noticeable red mark on her left cheek.

"Nonsense," Brett said, only, of course, he did not say *nonsense*, and he snarled what he did say. There was distinct discoloration across the bridge of his nose where it seemed the rope of pearls had struck him. "You did it deliberately, you drunken..." There followed more and cruder expletives.

But Klementina was not easily cowed and she replied in kind, at the top of her lungs. "Maybe I have a right to be angry," she concluded—not that it was the conclusion.

"Excuse me," Julian said tightly.

"Julian." Marguerite reached for him, but Julian ignored her, striding toward the center of the drama. "Oh, for God's sake," she murmured, and caught Ellery's arm when he moved to follow.

"No," she said. "Really. *No.*"

"Here comes momma's boy," Brett sneered as Julian reached him.

Julian hauled back his arm as though about to punch Brett, but Locke Lombard, the older gray-haired man Ellery had met earlier, interceded, aided by several other male guests who rushed to break up the fight that seemed imminent.

Ellery couldn't help wondering where Jack was. But it seemed the police chief's presence was unnecessary as Brett was hustled out into the garden without further incident.

Klementina, meanwhile, had retreated from the field of battle, sobbing loudly. A lifetime in theater had made Ellery a pretty good judge of tears, and he couldn't help thinking Klementina sounded more enraged than injured.

"*You'll be sorry*," she called.

Several of the other ladies stared after her, whispering behind their fans.

Marguerite let go of Ellery's arm. "I'm sorry. Julian is very protective of the people he cares for."

She seemed composed, smiling as though nothing had happened, although her gaze kept returning to the doorway Brett and his companions had vanished through.

"That's a nice quality in a man," Ellery said.

"It is." Marguerite's smile was briefer this time. "It's unnecessary in this case. I gave up worrying about how Brett's behavior might reflect on me or my family's name a long time ago. We're descended from pirates, after all."

Ellery smiled because that seemed to be the expected response. She couldn't really find it funny that her husband and his...whatever she was had started brawling in the middle of this fancy ball.

Marguerite gestured to the string quartet, which hastily began to play once more. People threw curious glances her way and at the door leading to the garden, but they began to laugh and talk again. Servants hurried to pick up the scattered pearls.

Marguerite let out a funny little laugh. "See? The excitement is all over."

"I'm sorry," Ellery said, unable to think of anything more useful to say.

She patted his arm. "You're sweet. Don't worry. We won't let this spoil the evening. Ah. There's Chief Carson. I guess it's true about never being able to find a cop when you need one."

Sure enough, Jack was making his way through the crowd.

"Excuse me, won't you, Ellery?" Marguerite moved to meet Locke, who had returned from the garden. Locke shook his head apologetically. He and Marguerite moved out of Ellery's view.

"What was that about?" a small, slim woman in purple asked Ellery.

It took him a moment to recognize acting mayor Nan Sweeny.

"I'm not exactly sure," he admitted. "Too many drinks?"

"I can guess. Kezzie's a fool if she thinks Brett is ever going to leave Marguerite."

Behind her purple lace mask, Nan was scowling.

Ellery stared. Like her aunt Nora, Nan seemed to have her ear to Pirate Cove's underground lines of communication.

"Is that what's going on?"

Nan shrugged. "It's usually what's going on with Brett. But if he thinks he can quietly brush Kezzie Harwood off, he's in for a rude awakening."

Kezzie—Klementina—did not seem like someone who would go quietly into the good night. Certainly she had not gone quietly tonight.

"Anyway. How are you? You look gorgeous. Are you having fun?" Nan asked.

"Yes. For sure," Ellery said. Which was mostly true.

They spoke for a few minutes longer, and then Nan went off to get another drink. Ellery decided to see if those crab puffs Nora had spoken of had materialized.

He was browsing the mostly empty silver trays—despite the recent burglary, the Bloodworths seemed in no danger of running out of sterling serving utensils—when Julian joined him.

"Here you are!" Julian was smiling widely, but Ellery couldn't help noticing that his hair was ruffled and his knuckles scraped.

"Hey," Ellery greeted him. "You okay?"

"Never better. Listen, I have to see about the fireworks. Are you all right on your own for a bit?"

"Of course." Ellery was amused. He also wondered if "see about the fireworks" was code, or if there really was going to be a fireworks show that evening.

Julian smiled winningly. "What I mean is, please don't run off. I'll be back as soon as I can."

"I'll be here."

Julian hesitated, then leaned in and gave Ellery a quick peck of a kiss, before turning away.

Ellery considered that kiss as he went upstairs to answer the call of nature. He decided it was really less of a true kiss and more of a social gesture, like a…a squeeze on the shoulder. Which was fine with him. He liked Julian and, even more, he liked the attention Julian was showering on him—it made a nice change— but he was definitely not looking for anything serious. And if he *had* been looking for something serious, it would probably not be with Julian, who he couldn't help feeling was a bit intense and, well, young. Never mind the fact that his family was more than a little complicated.

Eventually, Ellery located a bathroom, took care of necessities, and checked to make sure his costume was still intact and that he didn't have caviar stuck between his teeth.

He wandered amid the guests sprinkled like expensive party favors along the top level, and followed a small group out onto the balcony overlooking the garden and fountain. His heart gave a little jump as he spotted Jack down below, speaking with Sue Lewis.

He firmly redirected his attention as the fireworks display began, brilliant streams of glittering green and gold shooting across the night sky. His fellow guests, dressed like exiled kings and queens, stared out, *oohing* and *ahhing*.

Ellery moved to the edge of the balcony to see better.

The show was nearly over when a warm hand on his shoulder made him jump.

"Miss me?" Julian said softly.

Ellery turned and smiled. Yes, he was definitely enjoying the flirtation. Julian's admiration and flattery, while a bit much, were balm to his bruised ego. But he wasn't taking any of this seriously. He and Julian were from different worlds.

"Sure," he replied, and as Julian leaned in for a kiss, Ellery held up his champagne glass to his lips. "Is it true Captain Blood used to smuggle French champagne and Napoleon brandy along this coast?"

Julian blinked, gulped a mouthful of champagne, and laughed. "It's true. Better drink up. The ghost hunt is about to begin."

As he spoke, the great clock down in the main hall began to chime.

The crowd seemed to quiet as the slow, solemn strikes of the pendulum tolled the hour.

Midnight

CHAPTER EIGHT

There was no sign of either Brett or Klementina when Ellery and Julian joined the crowd gathered around Marguerite on the main floor.

Marguerite was speaking in that satiny contralto that seemed to carry without her ever having to raise her voice. "Those of you who've joined us in years past know the Marauder's Masquerade ball culminates with the annual ghost hunt at Seal Point. The old cemetery is within walking distance; however, depending on your choice of footwear, the going can be treacherous."

Ellery's feet twinged in anticipation. His toes felt pulverized, but no way was he going to miss the ghost hunt.

Marguerite smiled as though she could read the thought bubbles above all the bewigged heads. "For the adventurous among us, Julian will lead the way to Seal Point. For those of you who prefer to end the evening in comfort, I invite you to share midnight supper with me in the dining room."

There was a little round of applause.

It was instantly clear that the winner between the competing events was midnight supper with Marguerite—although Ellery noticed that a good portion of the fairly elderly crowd were skipping all further entertainments and lining up to wait their turn being chauffeured home in Sam Cuddlefish's limo.

Only a handful of the youngest guests followed Julian and Ellery out the Palladian doors and across the flagstone terrace, where the Fish and Chippies were packing up their instruments and sound system. The lights from the windows and doors of the mansion turned the lawns into a glowing checkerboard, and the costumed guests looked like shades of days gone by as they faded into the shadows of the garden.

Ellery couldn't resist glancing around to see what happened to Jack. He didn't spot him anywhere, so perhaps he was opting for schmoozing the local dignitaries over Cornish game hens and Napoleon brandy. Or maybe he'd already departed for home.

Though Ellery and Julian were in theory leading the way, they were quickly outdistanced by the more enthusiastic ghost hunters, most of them Julian's age or younger. Were these Julian's friends? If so, he seemed indifferent, even oblivious to them. And likewise.

"It's actually faster if we follow the drive and then cut through the old apple orchard to Seal Point," Julian was saying.

"That's fine with me. Should we—"

"They're fine." Julian was dismissive. "They'll find it."

They walked around the side of the house and started down the paved drive that Ellery and Dylan had hiked only a few hours earlier. Ellery looked around for Dylan, but it seemed he too had given a hard pass to the delights of stumbling around a graveyard at midnight.

Julian said, "Personally, I think the tradition of the ghost hunt began as a way to get people to go home after the ball."

Ellery made a sound of amusement. "So we're not going to see a ghost?"

"Do you believe in ghosts?"

"I don't know. Maybe. Probably."

Sam Cuddlefish's limo glided silently past, followed by several other cars honking cheerful goodnights. Julian raised a hand in automatic farewell.

"Do *you* believe in ghosts?" Ellery asked Julian when he showed no sign of breaking the silence that had fallen between them.

"Oh yes," Julian said quietly. "I believe in ghosts."

"Have you ever seen a ghost?"

Julian didn't answer as they moved farther to the side of the drive, making way as more guests found their cars and golf carts and began the precarious maneuver of backing up and turning around on such a narrow road.

They picked their way over stones and uneven ground, the beam of Julian's flashlight bobbing over the old rock wall and scattered wildflowers. As they strolled past Ellery's VW, he ignored the plea of his feet to call it a night.

In a matter of minutes, they had reached the end of the drive, and headed through what was left of the old apple orchard. The crooked smile of moon, the billowing sails of clouds, the gnarled and twisted trees created a fantasy landscape. Distant voices and laughter floated over the meadow behind the manor house. Flashlights flickered across the moonlit landscape like moths.

"Have you ever been here before?" Julian asked, holding the iron gate open for Ellery.

"No. It's not still in use, is it?"

Hinges screeched as the gate clanged shut.

Julian laughed. "It's still in *use*, but there are currently no vacancies."

"Right. That's what I meant."

"My mother will be buried here, of course. And in time I will be too. And my husband, I suppose. We'll go into the family crypt, though. Not the ground."

"This is getting depressing," Ellery said. He was teasing, but the conversation did seem a little macabre.

"Do you think so?" Julian sounded surprised.

By that point their fellow ghost hunters had caught up. Nervous giggles and low whispers drifted through the stone crosses and headstones as the others scattered around graves in the quest to find Tom Blood—or any other ghost hanging around on a Saturday night. Flashlight beams bounced off mossy statuary and cut swaths through the misty air like misdirected signal lights.

"Is there a prize for the person who spots Tom Blood's ghost first?" Ellery asked.

Julian chuckled. "No. Having your wits scared out of you should be reward enough."

No kidding.

The old cemetery with its stained monuments and overgrown gravestones was pretty creepy. An eerie energy seemed to hang in the damp air. The scent of wet earth, cold marble, and mold vied with the distant breeze. Every rustle of bushes or crack of twigs sent a prickle of unease down Ellery's spine.

"BOO!" someone shouted in the dark, and a couple of girls screamed and then burst into laughter.

Ellery wondered sadly if he was actually too old for ghost hunting.

From the other side of the cemetery, someone called, "Hey! Hey, guys, I think I found his grave! Over here, guys!"

Several shadows peeled off and went stumbling over gravestones and clumps of sea grass to see.

"Where? Where are you?"

"Here! Behind the weeping angel."

"Did you want to—" Ellery began.

Julian shook his head. "He's not buried over there." His smile was odd in the moonlight. "That's Thomas Bloodworth the Third. Captain Blood isn't buried anywhere. He went down with his ship—the *Blood Red Rose*."

"That's right." Ellery remembered Nora's story of how Blood's young bride had jumped into the ocean after his ship sank.

Julian said dreamily, "According to legend, the *Blood Red Rose* rises from the sea on the first clear full moon after the summer solstice. She sails into the Buccaneer's Bay, all misty silver like a cloud, and you can see Captain Blood walking her decks."

"That would be something to see," Ellery agreed. "Do the sightings only occur on the first clear moon after the solstice?"

"Yes. And when a member of the Bloodworth clan dies."

Yikes.

"Then if we're not hunting for Captain Blood, who are we hunting for?"

Julian shrugged. "We've got lots of family ghosts." He added meaningfully, "And lots of family skeletons."

"Ha." Ellery didn't doubt it.

"Besides. The Bloodworths don't have a monopoly on the spirits in this graveyard. You can take your pick."

"Believe it or not, I'm not up on all the ghosts in Pirate's Cove."

"To start with, there's John Mansfield and Ann Rathbone. Rathbone jumped into the sea near Skull House after murdering Mansfield."

"Okay, yes, I'm familiar with that story."

"Of course. You solved the murder of Brandon Abbott."

"Yeeah," Ellery said uncomfortably. "I wouldn't really say—"

Julian wasn't listening. "There's Rufus Blackwell. He was betrayed by his brother and hung in 1723. If you want more recent ghosts, there's Tristan Wallace, the multimillionaire oil-and-gas magnate who disappeared off his boat about twenty years ago right off this coast. His ghost is supposed to haunt the harbor pier."

"You certainly know a lot about the island's ghosts."

Julian said, "Yes. One of these days, I'm planning to write a book about all Buck Island's hauntings."

Ellery smiled. "Great. You can have your first signing at the Crow's Nest."

"I would love that." Julian wrapped his arm around Ellery's shoulders and gave him a quick hug. He whispered, "You want to see the family crypt?"

Ellery laughed. As romantic invitations went, Julian could afford to brush up on his technique. "Um, well... Don't you want to look for some ghosts?"

"We can look up there." Julian pointed to the small marble structure atop the hillock. "There's a bench with a perfect view of the cove. If Captain Blood *should* decide to make an appearance tonight, we'll have a front row view."

"Wouldn't that mean someone in the Bloodworth clan has to die?"

Julian said bleakly, "I can think of someone I wouldn't mind not seeing at breakfast tomorrow. Not that he's ever up for breakfast."

Ellery had no response to that, and he didn't resist the gentle tug Julian gave him.

They wandered through the headstones, not speaking. Julian seemed to know his way even in the dark. That wasn't exactly amazing. Not only was his family buried here, he had probably played in the old cemetery growing up. Kids would find it a cool place, with all the old statues of marble angels and robed mourners and tall stone crosses.

"What's that?" someone called from a few yards away.

"Where?"

"Over there. I see a figure."

"It's just the mist."

"No. No, look. It's a figure. By that stone coffin. It's moving. It's trying to hide!"

Ellery began, "I think they mean us—"

But his words were cut off as Julian kissed him.

It wasn't totally a surprise. He could hardly have missed Julian's continued efforts to position himself, the octopusian meanderings of his arm, the way he leaned in and out as he tried to decide between whispering sweet nothings or just going for it. Inevitably, he was going to go for it, and Ellery was okay with that. They were in a pretty good place for it, sheltered as they were between a stalwart bronze of one of Pirate Cove's founding fathers and a narrow tomb about the size of a small toolshed.

Ellery liked Julian and found him attractive, but he had pretty much already made up his mind that Julian was not for him. The last half hour of wandering through the graveyard while Julian made cryptic pronouncements had cemented his feelings.

However, he was curious, so he let Julian kiss him—and he kissed Julian back.

It was nice. A sweet kiss. Julian was eager but tentative, and even when he got encouragement, he was very gentle, maybe a little shy. There was nothing not to like in that warm, diffident press of mouth to mouth.

"I can't believe you're really here," Julian whispered when their lips parted.

Which, frankly, neither could Ellery. Not that he hadn't done plenty of kissing in graveyards—those scenes were a staple of the *Happy Halloween! You're Dead* flicks—but it was definitely different with lights and reflectors and cameras and crew.

He opened his mouth to say something tactful when, just like in the *Happy Halloween! You're Dead* movies, a figure seemed to materialize from the shadows. However, unlike in the movies, it was not a vengeful ghost or an ax-wielding maniac. Oh no, it was much worse.

It was Jack.

Julian jumped guiltily. "I didn't see you there, Chief!"

Jack ignored him. "Man overboard?" he suggested to Ellery. His tone was wry.

Where did *Jack* get off being wry about Ellery's dating decisions? Ellery demanded, "What the heck are you doing lurking there, Jack?"

"Trying to avoid the two of you." Jack sounded nettled, "And I wasn't *lurking*. I tried clearing my throat."

"I-I thought you were a yellow-crowned night heron…" Julian faltered, and Ellery began to splutter.

Jack, being Jack, couldn't be discomfited for long. Even so, there was a note of something in his curt, "Apologies. I didn't mean to intrude." His figure melted into the shadows.

Was that *hurt* he heard in Jack's tone? No way. Not Jack.

It took Julian a moment to regain his composure. He gave a shaky chuckle. "He scared the hell out of me. I thought he was Captain Blood's ghost for sure."

Ellery forced a laugh. It was a ridiculous situation, yet he felt awkward, almost guilty. Which made no sense, given how clearly Jack had indicated he wasn't interested in kissing Ellery.

Julian captured Ellery's hand again, and they continued up the stone walk to the baroque marble structure at the top.

The Bloodworth crypt was larger than Ellery had expected. In fact, it was technically a mausoleum, with half the structure built underground. The aboveground portion was a grand design of square columns and curved walls. A pair of weirdly devious-looking angels seemed to shelter in the two front niches flanking the arched stone door within its dim recess.

"*Ta-da,*" said Julian.

It occurred to Ellery that he had never visited Great-great-great-aunt Eudora's or any of his family's graves. He did not even know where the Pages were buried. In fact, for all he knew, the early Pages might be scattered somewhere amid the tombstones of Seal Point.

"You can see right down into the cove from here." Julian pointed to the starlit waves foaming on the beach far below. "The *Blood Red Rose* used to anchor there, where no one could see her."

"Wouldn't the water be too shallow?"

"You'd think so, but I guess there's a way in, if you know it."

"Or maybe that's just a legend," Ellery said.

Julian shrugged, turned back to study the moonlit structure. "What do you think of it?"

"It's...impressive."

"My father's buried here."

"Oh, I thought..." Actually, what had he thought? He had assumed Julian's father and mother were divorced.

"I don't really remember him. He was a lot older than my mother. And he was sick."

"How old were you when he passed?"

"Four," Julian said.

This was an unexpected bond between them. "I was seven when my dad died," Ellery said. "I remember him, but not as well as I'd like to."

Julian stared at him. "Did your mother remarry?"

"Yes. George, my stepdad, has been...well, I love him. He *is* my dad."

"You're lucky."

Thinking of Brett Ainsley, Ellery had to agree. "So?"

Ellery repeated cautiously, "So?"

"Want to peek inside?"

"Not really," Ellery said honestly.

Julian laughed. "You made all those scary movies, and you don't want to look inside a real live crypt?"

"Mausoleum," Ellery corrected. "Crypts are the underground vault part."

Julian stared. "That's a weird thing to know."

Ellery shrugged. "Like you said, I've been in a lot of scary movies."

"True. Come on. You'll like this. The statues are covered in gold leaf, and the ceiling is painted with ships and sea monsters. It's really cool."

Ellery opened his mouth to decline the pleasures of exploring the family crypt—er, mausoleum—but Julian went up the steps to the stone door.

"If you twist the head of the mermaid on the ship's figurehead, it releases the spring…" He stepped back as the heavy door slid silently open.

"Cool, right?"

"That's pretty cool," Ellery agreed. Figuratively and literally. The building seemed to exhale in a gasp of chilly, grave-scented air.

Julian smiled back at him. "No electric lights, but there are oil lamps."

"I hope you're kidding."

"I brought a lighter. And we have the flashlight." Julian shone the beam briefly around the inky interior. The beam seemed to catch the glitter of eyes and then move on.

"What was *that*?" Ellery said.

"Eleanor." Julian stepped inside the mausoleum. "The first Mrs. Captain Blood. Her statue, I mean." His voice faded.

The hair rose on the back of Ellery's neck in an instant atavistic response. He did *not* want to step inside that building. Elliot Parker had not survived six gruesome installments of *Happy Halloween! You're Dead* by accident.

"Hey, you know what? I don't think this is a good idea."

"Are you afraid?" Julian was laughing as he turned. "Are you afraid of *ghosts*?"

"Am I afraid to go exploring a haunted pirate crypt in an old graveyard at midnight? Is that a serious question?"

"It's not a crypt, remember? It's a—" Julian seemed to tumble and then stagger forward, losing his balance. "What the—" he began in a strange tone, and then his voice died away.

"Julian?" Ellery sprang to the threshold, peering into the darkness. "Are you okay?"

Silence.

"Julian?"

No. Not silence. He could hear Julian breathing—breathing strangely, heavily.

"Not funny, Julian," Ellery snapped. His eyes strained in the pitchy interior, trying to discern Julian's crouched figure from the statues ringing the center of the room.

Julian had dropped his flashlight when he'd tripped. Ellery saw movement near the wall and the flashlight switched on, illuminating a tiled mosaic floor and the base of a pedestal.

"Are you all right?" They had both done a fair bit of drinking that evening, but Ellery didn't suspect Julian of being drunk so much as being a jerk. He'd had experience with people who thought that because Ellery had been the star of a successful horror movie franchise, it was hysterical to try and scare the wits out of him.

"Yes. I thought I felt something…" Julian's voice quavered.

The white beam of the flashlight rolled slowly around the floor of the mausoleum, picking out dried leaves, a pistol, and eyes. Not painted. Not jeweled. Human. Dead, staring human eyes in a dead, waxy human face.

"Jesus Christ!" Julian shot out of the darkness and into Ellery's arms. "It's Brett," he babbled, clutching Ellery. "He's *dead*."

CHAPTER NINE

Ellery sucked in a sharp breath.

This was not the first dead body he'd encountered. It was not even the first dead body in pirate's costume he'd found. That didn't make it any better.

In some ways, it made it worse. As bad habits went, this was one he *really* didn't want to develop.

He fumbled for the flashlight Julian still held, and pointed it in the direction of the body. Brett Ainsley stared sightlessly back at him.

"Oh my God."

How? Why? Okay, *why* was probably a dumb question. But how? Just a few minutes earlier they'd seen Brett being escorted outside. How had he wound up a corpse in a closed crypt—er, mausoleum—half a mile away. Ellery's thoughts were a confused jumble. He felt shocked and a little sick, the image of the dead man seeming to burn itself onto the retina of his memory.

Julian freed himself, lurched forward again, blocking Ellery's view for a moment. He whispered, "He killed himself..." He bent to retrieve the pistol.

"Don't touch it!" Ellery warned.

But Julian had already picked up the pistol. He stared at it, stared stupidly at Ellery, and then dropped the pistol from nerveless fingers. It clanged on the tile floor.

"Fingerprints," he said dully. "I forgot."

"You *forgot*?" Ellery repeated in disbelief.

Forgot? How the heck could Julian—a professed mystery buff—*forget* about fingerprints?

"I didn't think." Julian looked around the gloomy chamber as though searching for an answer. "I don't understand..."

Ellery stepped back from the entrance of the mausoleum and felt for his phone in the cavernous pocket of his velvet frock coat. At the same time, he was shouting, "*Jack?* Jack, can you hear me?" There was no reason to believe Jack was still within earshot. It was just...instinct. Or possibly wishful thinking. "Jack, we've got a situation here."

He scrolled through his contacts, found Jack's number, even as people in the lower part of the cemetery began to cry out, "What's wrong? Where are you?"

"Help! Help!" Julian yelled from inside the mausoleum. Which really didn't help matters.

The phone began to ring on the other end just as the pound of footfalls on damp earth reached his ears. Someone was coming up the hill fast—someone whose cell phone was ringing.

"Ellery?" Jack called. He sounded slightly out of breath.

"Here. Over here." Ellery turned to Julian, who was still shouting. "Stop that!"

Jack's silhouette topped the rise a second before Jack. Ellery went to meet him.

"What's wrong?"

Inside the mausoleum, Julian stopped yelling as abruptly as he'd begun.

Ellery blurted, "Brett Ainsley's dead."

"*Dead?*"

"We found him in the mausoleum. I think he's been shot."

Jack barely checked, striding past Ellery toward the mausoleum. Ellery followed.

"Stay back," Jack warned him.

"Don't worry," Ellery muttered. Compared to his reaction the first time he'd bumbled over a body, he was relatively composed. He didn't feel composed, though. He felt sick and shocked. He wished he had not had so much champagne. He wished he had not eaten so many lobster toasts. He wished he had not gone ghost-hunting with Julian Bloodworth.

Jack flicked his flashlight beam first on Julian, who stood motionless by the gold statue of a monk, then on Brett. It was not a pretty sight. There were ominous dark splotches over the front of Brett's blue-velvet doublet. His face was slack and stupid, eyes staring in surprise.

Jack gave a startled exclamation and squatted down beside the corpse.

"I can't believe this," Julian said. "What was he doing here?"

Given the pool of blood soaking the tiles? Dying. But Ellery didn't answer. All his attention was on Jack's quick, cursory examination.

Jack shook his head, rose. "He's still warm."

"Well, he would be," Ellery said. "We saw him alive only a little while ago." Was that right? Come to think of it, how many hours *had* passed since Brett had been ushered outside to cool off? One? Two? It was like time had stopped from the moment he'd walked through the doors of Blood House.

Anyway, didn't it take about twelve hours for a body to cool to the touch?

"This can't be happening," Julian protested.

Neither Ellery nor Jack bothered replying.

"Did either of you touch anything in here?"

"I picked up the gun," Julian said.

"Y—" Jack cut off the rest of it. He looked at Ellery.

"No," Ellery said. "I might have rested my hand on the entrance. I don't remember."

"All right. It's going to take some time to get a crime-scene team up here. I need you to round up everyone below and get them back to the house. No one is to leave until we've got everyone's statements."

"Right. Okay."

"I'll phone ahead, but I want to make sure nothing gets lost in translation."

Ellery nodded.

"Julian, go with him."

Julian assented dully.

"Come on, Julian," Ellery said.

It turned out that no real rounding up was required. The remaining ghost hunters were climbing up the hillock as Ellery and Julian started down.

"There's been an accident," Ellery answered the calls for information. "We're all supposed to go back to the manor and wait."

"What kind of accident?" a woman called.

"The fatal kind, obviously," someone else returned.

"Chief Carson thinks I did it," Julian muttered.

"Don't say that." Ellery threw a quick, uneasy glance at their companions.

"It's true. He thinks I shot Brett."

"No, of course not," Ellery said, although he wasn't so sure.

"I saw his expression."

"Why did you pick up the gun?" Ellery asked.

"Instinct."

Ellery was trying to be understanding, but he couldn't help the note of exasperation that crept in.

"What instinct would make you pick up a possible murder weapon?"

Julian's voice rose. "I don't know. I was in shock."

Ellery didn't press any further. For one thing, they were getting strange looks from their fellow ghost hunters. For another, he thought Julian probably *was* in shock. Because what else could explain his behavior?

* * * * *

Ellery's memories of what happened once they got back to Bloodworth Manor were hazy.

Most of the Masquerade guests had departed not long after the ghost hunt had begun. About twenty die-hards were enjoying a cold supper in the stately dining room when the police arrived—which was a few minutes after Ellery and Julian led their party inside.

Julian had gone straight to his mother, which was understandable, though Ellery knew Jack would have liked to forestall that. Ellery was now an experienced enough connoisseur of mystery to know that the police liked to observe their prime-suspects' reactions upon learning of a sudden death, and Marguerite, as the spouse of the murdered man, *had* to be the number-one suspect.

When the police showed up, the remaining guests had been shepherded into this large, formal dining room. Stoic-looking servers provided coffee and tea and pastries, though no one seemed to have much appetite. A young officer, Jack's latest recruit, stood inside the room, silent and expressionless as he watched everyone and no doubt took mental notes for his chief.

It would be interesting to know what the fresh-faced, earnest Officer Battye made of this cast of suspects. Ellery wasn't sure what *he* made of them.

As grieving widows went, Mrs. Bloodworth-Ainsley seemed somber but composed. She had removed her mask—they were all maskless by then—and her face was colorless and drawn. There was no sign of tears, but Ellery was guessing she was someone who preferred to do her weeping in private.

Or her not-weeping in private.

As far as prime suspects went, Julian would be running a close second to Marguerite.

To Ellery's eye, Julian looked haggard and withdrawn. Which was normal and understandable.

What was not normal or understandable, what continued to nag at Ellery, was why he'd picked up that gun even as Ellery had told him *not* to? Okay, shock. But why had he insisted on going up to the mausoleum in the first place? The view. Okay. But then why had he insisted on opening up the mausoleum?

Ellery wanted to believe it was all innocent, an unfortunate series of coincidences, sheer bad luck, but the problem with reading as many mystery novels as he'd been reading over the past five months was it made you suspicious, skeptical, even cynical.

And if *he* was feeling unwillingly suspicious, skeptical, and cynical, Jack would be feeling all of that multiplied by ten.

But just the little he had observed of Brett Ainsley that evening made Ellery think there would be plenty of suspects outside the immediate family circle. Plenty of suspects who might be sitting right at that very table.

Not all of them, though.

He remembered Nan Sweeny implying that Klementina Harwood was having an affair with Brett—and that she was not his first nor would be his last. Klementina and Brett had had a very public altercation mid-masquerade, so absolutely Kezzie Harwood had to be high on that list of suspects.

Klementina had left the party early—and noisily—but that didn't mean she hadn't met up with Brett later. Granted, a mausoleum was a weird place for a rendezvous and, as it turned out, not as private as you might think.

Maybe there was a Mr. Harwood? He'd be on the list of suspects too.

There would be business associates and social acquaintances. There would be other family members perhaps? Maybe Brett came from a long line of homicidal maniacs. That would be convenient. Ex-girlfriends? Poker buddies? Brett looked like a guy who would cheat at cards as readily as at love.

Maybe he'd made enemies at his yacht club? Or on his polo team?

Ellery had no idea whether Brett sailed a yacht or played polo. He'd had a certain Ralph- Lauren-on-the-Skids style. For sure, he did not look like a guy who worked nine-to-five, but it seemed unlikely that most guests at the evening's events were punching time clocks.

Ellery glanced automatically around the crowded dining table and saw Julian watching him. Julian offered a nervous smile. Ellery smiled back.

Yeah, he was worried about Julian.

Julian's knuckles had been skinned when he came back from helping escort Brett outside for some fresh air. Had there been some kind of fight outside?

Who would know?

Locke Lombard would know. He had stopped Julian from punching Brett after the scene with Klementina.

Ellery looked for Locke and spotted him sitting next to Marguerite. Their heads were bent close together, and they were speaking quietly. Marguerite had stuck to the "accident" excuse when she'd informed her guests they would have to wait for the police before departing, but it was a safe bet Locke knew the true story. He had Trusted Family Friend written all over him.

Had Brett reappeared inside after the incident with Klementina?

Ellery tried to remember seeing him, but he was drawing a blank.

In fairness, a lot of the evening was beginning to feel fuzzy and far away. He checked his phone and nearly dropped it.

Three o'clock?

In the morning?

Poor little Watson would think he had been abandoned again. He hated being crated. All the fuzzy pillows, soft lights, and YouTube videos in the world couldn't soothe him. Whenever Ellery was forced to leave him in the cage, he inevitably returned to Watson having barked himself hoarse with outrage and hurt.

"How much longer?" a woman in a pink bee-hive-sized wig asked.

Marguerite opened her eyes, opened her mouth, but was forestalled by the dining-room door opening. Jack walked in.

Somewhere along the way, Jack had changed out of costume and back into his navy uniform. He was courteous but crisp. "Thanks for your patience, folks. We're going to make this as painless as possible."

After that, things happened very quickly. The remaining guests were divided into two groups. The larger group went with Detective Lansing. The rest continued to wait in the dining room to be inter-viewed by Police Chief Carson.

Ellery, one of those requested to wait in the din-ing room, couldn't help noticing that though Lansing took charge of the larger group, Jack's detainees included Marguerite, Julian, Locke, and the other men who had helped break up the fight between Brett and Kezzie. All the prime suspects.

He hoped Jack was not including him in the category of prime suspect, or that was *really* going to place a strain on their friendship.

Another strain.

The male guests who had interceded between Brett and Kezzie were picked off one by one in quick succession.

Then Locke was called. He rose, grave and dignified in his eighteenth-century King's Counsel wig and black gown, squeezed Marguerite's shoulder lightly, and left the room. Julian shifted over to take his place. He and Marguerite spoke softly, briefly, then fell silent.

Julian looked down the table at Ellery. "Sorry about this."

"No worries," Ellery said, which was hardly accurate.

Officer Battye, stationed at the door, said apologetically, "You're not supposed to compare notes."

Julian frowned. "We're not comparing notes. I'm apologizing to my date for ruining his evening."

Marguerite murmured, "Julian."

Julian folded his lips together in a sullen line. He met Ellery's gaze and shook his head.

According to Ellery's phone, it was forty minutes before the door to the dining room opened and Officer Martin looked around the almost empty room and called, "Ellery Page?" as if he didn't know Ellery perfectly well—right down to how he took his coffee.

Ellery rose, nodded farewell to his remaining hosts, and followed Martin through the dining room door and across the now empty main room. The grand chandelier was dark, the candles had been doused, the flowers were looking wilted around the edges, and one of Kezzie's lost pearls gleamed between the toes of a claw-foot table.

They turned down a short, shining marble hall, Martin pushed open a door, and Ellery stepped inside an elegant blue sitting room.

Jack was seated at a small writing table. He was rubbing the back of his neck, but he straightened and squared his shoulders at the sight of Ellery.

"Thanks, Martin." Jack motioned at the Louis XVI green-upholstered chair in front of the writing table. "Have a seat."

Ellery dropped into the chair and studied Jack. He thought Jack looked as tired and drawn as Marguerite. This was bound to be a tricky case for Jack. Murder among the summer folk? Not just summer folk—one of the oldest and richest families on the island.

Jack would call it "politically sensitive," which Ellery translated to mean potential pitfalls every way Jack stepped.

Jack reached for his cell phone on the desktop, hesitated, asked, "You okay?"

"Me? Yes. I'm fine."

Jack nodded, pressed his phone, said, "Interview with Ellery Page, Sunday, July 11." He glanced at his watch. "4:10 a.m."

Ellery said nothing.

"Okay," Jack said, sounding weary but still brisk. "I think I know the answer to these initial questions, but let's just verify. How long have you known Brett Ainsley?"

"I met him for the first time this evening. I think we exchanged all of a sentence."

"And your relationship to Julian Bloodworth?"

"I met Julian for the first time this evening also. We hung out together for most of the party."

"That's what I'm interested in," Jack said. "That timeline." He jotted something on his notepad and glanced up. "Were you ever apart during the course of the evening?"

"Of course we were apart."

Jack ignored Ellery's flash of exasperation. "Of course. So let's start with your best estimate of when you met Julian, and then we'll track your movements from there."

"My movements or Julian's?" Ellery asked.

Jack said blandly, "If you know where Julian was when he wasn't with you, feel free to share."

Okay. Point taken.

Ellery thought back. "Dylan and I arrived about the same time. That would have been slightly after seven. I met Marguerite and Brett, I milled around, talked to some people, avoided talking to some people, ran into Dylan again and we went outside to the bar, where I met Julian."

"What time was that?"

"Honestly, I don't know. But Brett was still alive because when we walked inside, we saw him fooling around with Klementina Harwood. She was sitting on his lap, and he was trying to stick his tongue in her ear."

Jack remained impassive. "And what was Julian's reaction to that?"

Ellery sighed. "I don't think he liked it. Who would?"

"Did he speak to Brett?"

"No. That was right after we ran into you, so maybe that helps you pinpoint the time." He remembered he'd gotten snarky and Jack had gotten distant and cool, but it felt long ago. Though not as long ago as the easy camaraderie of their lunch Tuesday afternoon. That felt like another lifetime.

"Did you remember something?" Jack's lashes flicked up. He regarded Ellery closely.

Ellery shook his head. "No. We—Julian and I—were going to find somewhere we could talk and actually hear each other, but we kept running into people. At one point we stepped back out to get another drink and listen to the band."

"How was Julian's mood?"

Ellery considered Jack for a moment. "Romantic."

Jack's eyes flickered. "Did he talk about Brett?"

"Nope."

"Right. So you spent how long listening to the band and being romantic?"

"We weren't—" Ellery stopped. "It must have been around 11:30…maybe? I'm not at all clear about the time. I know we came inside and Julian introduced me to his mother."

"I thought you'd already met Marguerite?"

"I had. It was just…a sweet gesture."

"Huh," Jack said in the tone of one who was naturally distrustful of sweet gestures. "There was an altercation at 11:35."

This was the part Ellery really didn't want to get into. "Yes. I'm not exactly sure what happened. Klementina Harwood was swinging her pearls around, kind of like a pretend stripper, and she must've hit Brett in the face. I'm not sure if he thought she did it on purpose or what, but he slapped her."

Jack made a check mark against his notes, so this appeared to confirm something he already knew.

"Go on," he murmured.

"They were both really drunk. Julian went to talk to them, and…"

"And?"

Ellery half closed his eyes, trying to remember. It had all happened so fast. But if he viewed the scuffle as movements in a choreographed fight sequence?

He said slowly, "I think Brett was the aggressor."

Jack stopped writing. "It's important to get this sequence of events right. You're saying Brett attacked Julian without provocation?"

Once again, Ellery replayed the events of earlier in his mind. He grimaced. "No. I think...Brett said something to Julian—"

"What did he say?"

"Momma's boy? Something idiotic. And Julian reacted—"

"Reacted how?"

Ellery considered his words, but it was all going to come out anyway. "He started to throw a punch, but Locke Lombard stepped in. I think Brett pushed Locke or tried to get around him to Julian, but everybody jumped in and hurried Brett outside."

"Then what?"

"Well, Klementina was crying and yelling that he couldn't treat her that way and he hadn't seen the last of her. I'm amazed you didn't hear her. Then she stormed off. You showed up. That was pretty much the end of it. I ran into Mayor Sweeny, and we chatted for a while."

"How long before you saw Julian again?"

Ellery sighed. "You know, I had a lot to drink tonight, Jack. I wasn't watching the clock."

"I get that," Jack said, "but the timeline here is important. If you can be more accurate, that could be helpful to Julian."

Or it could be *not* helpful to Julian. But Ellery didn't say that. No need to state the obvious.

"It couldn't have been too long. He came back for a minute to tell me he had to make sure everything was ready for the fireworks display. He said he'd be right back."

"How did Julian seem at that point?"

"He seemed fine. Apologetic." Ellery searched for the word. "Solicitous."

Jack's gaze did that little flicker again.

"I went upstairs, the fireworks started, and Julian joined me on the balcony not too long after that. There were a bunch of other people up there, and I'm sure someone will have noticed the time."

The time Julian joined them. Not the amount of time he was gone. And naturally, it was the latter Jack was interested in.

"Did you see Brett at any time after Julian went to check on the fireworks display?"

Ellery had known that question was coming. He didn't want to answer, but lying was not an option. "No."

"Did you see him at any time after he went outside with Julian and the others?"

"No, but there *were* others. It wasn't like Brett and Julian went out there on their own."

Jack was watching him closely. "After Julian joined you on the balcony, did you remain together until the ghost hunt began?"

"Yes."

"You're sure?"

"Yes. Absolutely."

Jack leaned back in his chair. His tone was neutral as he asked, "What was Julian's mood when he joined you on the balcony? How did he seem?"

Calls for speculation on the part of the witness, Your Honor! But this was an investigation, not a trial, and Jack had to begin somewhere. In this case, he had to rely on the observations of every potential witness.

"He seemed fine. He seemed…playful. In good spirits." Ellery added, "He sure didn't seem like he'd been running through a graveyard. He wasn't disheveled. He didn't have any blood on his clothes. He seemed fine. Normal."

He thought about Julian's grazed knuckles. Jack would notice those for himself when he interviewed Julian. Ellery didn't have to go out of his way to point the finger of suspicion.

Jack tapped his pencil on his notepad for a second or two. He said finally, "Whose idea was it to walk up to the mausoleum?"

Ellery admitted, "His." He added quickly, "He said the view of the cove was better up there, and it was."

"Whose idea was it to open and enter the mausoleum?"

"His."

Jack was relentless. "Who discovered the body?"

Ellery sighed. "Julian did."

Jack nodded, made a final note, glanced up at Ellery. "Thanks. That's all. You're free to leave."

Ellery opened his mouth, saw a certain bleakness in Jack's gaze, and swallowed his words.

CHAPTER TEN

Ellery woke to golden sunlight, a cold wet nose in his ear, and the buzz of his cell phone.

He blinked, trying to orient himself. His mouth tasted like the moldy linoleum he and Jack had ripped up in the kitchen, his thinking was fuzzy, and he had a definite headache. It had been so long since he'd had a hangover, it took him a few seconds to recognize the symptoms.

Ugh.

Watson moaned as though he too was suffering ill effects from the night before, and burrowed his head more firmly into Ellery's neck.

What day was it? Sunday, right? Usually, his day off. Except he'd made a big point to Jack about how he wouldn't be taking Sundays off until the fall. Clearly, a lapse in sanity. *Hell yes*, he was taking Sundays off. He was sure as heck taking *this* Sunday off. He closed his eyes. He was going to lie here and sleep for as long as he needed to. And today he needed to. And Watson needed him to. Watson had had a rough night too.

"Poor little buddy," he murmured.

Watson muttered agreement.

Ellery was surprised at how much he enjoyed waking up with the warm ball of Watson snuggled against his chest or his back. Not as much as he'd enjoyed waking up to Todd when things between them had been good, true, but it was very comforting. Comforting and comfortable. He'd replaced the antique bed's old sagging mattress two weeks earlier with a custom-made supportive and cushiony hybrid, and he was getting some of the best sleep he'd had in months. The nights were warm enough to leave the windows open, and the songs of morning birds and summery scent of the meadow floated in. It was very peaceful. His eyelids drifted shut.

His cell phone buzzed again.

Ellery frowned. Opened his eyes. Was there a problem at the Crow's Nest? It was hard to imagine anything coming up that Nora couldn't handle.

"Sorry, buddy." He reached past Watson, found his phone, peered blearily at the screen.

Yikes.

Ten o'clock in the morning!

A string of missed calls greeted his alarmed gaze.

Unknown number.

Unknown number.

Nora.

Dylan.

Editor@Scuttlebuttweekly.

Nora.

Dylan.

Unknown Number.

"What the…"

Ellery checked for messages. There were several.

"Ellery, dearie, I've just read the terrible news in this morning's paper." Nora's recorded voice pierced his mental fog. "Such a shock for you. Are you coming in today? Should we prepare a statement for the press?"

Ellery felt a sinking feeling much akin to what Captain Blood must have experienced as the salty waters closed over his head. He scrolled to the next message, pressed Play.

Dylan's plummy voice filled his ear. "What in the world happened last night? Is it true? You found Brett's body in the family mausoleum? Were you there when Julian was arrested? Surely you're not under suspicion *again*. Call me!"

Watson sat up and yawned. Even his yawns were noisy, his jaws opening as wide as a Muppet's as he squeaked out his morning song. His big brown eyes seemed to smile at Ellery. He wagged his tail.

"Good morning to you too," Ellery murmured. "I hope we don't have to go on the lam with *that* singing voice."

He braced himself and pressed to play the message from Editor@Scuttlebuttweekly.

"Hi, Ellery, Sue Lewis here. I'm personally reaching out to invite you to give your statement regarding the arrest of your boyfriend, Julian Bloodworth. We don't want any accusations that we haven't been fair to you or that we're attempting to try you in the court of public opinion. Get back to me ASAP. We go to print at midnight, with or without your statement."

Sure, Sue. I'll get right on that.

His sense of trepidation grew as he stared at the final message, the message from an unknown number. He pressed Play.

"I didn't do it, Ellery." Julian's voice wavered. "I'm not a murderer. You have to know that. You were there. You know I'm innocent. You have to help me. You're the only one who can. Please. I'm depending on you."

The message clicked off. Ellery played it again.

What the hell… Had Jack really arrested Julian? Less than twenty-four hours into his investigation? That wasn't like Jack. Jack wasn't an open-and-shut kind of cop. What had made him decide Brett Ainsley's murder was an open-and-shut kind of case? It would have to be more than he had learned from Ellery the night before.

And Julian… Ellery's heart sank. What did Julian think Ellery could do for him? He had already supplied him with as much of an alibi as he truthfully could.

"You have to help me. You're the only one who can."

Julian needed a good lawyer, not a mystery bookseller. And it was safe to assume Marguerite Bloodworth would hire the best legal team money could buy. Unless…

Did Julian's mother believe he had killed her husband?

Ellery considered that for a moment.

Perhaps she did. Perhaps she blamed Julian. Ellery didn't know any of these people, including Julian, well enough to make any assumptions, but if he was going by his impressions of the night before—facial expressions, body language, tone of voice, all the things he had learned as an actor to pay close attention to—he would have bet that, even if Marguerite believed Julian had murdered Brett, she would never turn her back on her son.

Which just made this all the more confusing.

"Please. I'm depending on you."

"But why?" Ellery protested. "Why depend on *me*?"

Watson's tail stirred.

It wasn't that Ellery didn't want to help. He did. He liked Julian. He'd had a nice time being Julian's surprise date for the Marauder's Masquerade. He had enjoyed all the appreciation and admiration being showered on him. Enjoyed it as a change of menu. Not as a steady diet. He had not ended the evening believing he and Julian were destined for true love.

In fact, he had ended the evening pretty sure he and Julian were *not* destined for anything more than possible friendship.

For one thing, Julian was too young for him. However old he was, he was too young for Ellery. And for another, he was, well, not quite on Ellery's wavelength. Ellery wasn't looking to be idolized. He wanted to be valued, sure; respected, of course. But he wasn't looking for a fan. He was looking for—well, he wasn't *looking* for anything, which was another point.

What if it was Jack looking for more? What if it was Jack looking for a relationship? whispered his subconscious.

Ellery squelched that little voice. It *wasn't* Jack looking for more. Jack had made it very clear, painfully clear, he wasn't looking for anything more. Besides, Ellery had been open to exploring *possibilities* with Jack. That was all. He hadn't been ready to commit to anything more than that.

(And by the way, Jack had *plenty* of flaws of his own. Ellery wasn't forgetting about Jack leaving him to freeze in the Barbys' icehouse just to teach him a lesson.)

But the real reason, the main reason Ellery didn't want Julian depending on him was because Ellery was not one hundred percent sure Julian *hadn't* killed Brett.

He hated to even think it, but it was the truth.

He didn't believe Julian had killed Brett—he really didn't—but would he want to bet his life on it? No. He wouldn't.

It didn't seem plausible that Julian would pick the night of the Marauder's Masquerade to commit murder. But *someone* had decided to commit murder that night.

And it would *have* to be premeditated, right? To get Brett to leave the party and go down to the mausoleum would require advance planning.

Which maybe limited the cast of suspects.

It would eliminate Klementina Harwood, for example.

Unless, she had staged that brawl with Brett.

But what would her motive be?

That was always the question, wasn't it? What was anyone's motive? Including Julian's.

Presumably, if Jack had gone so far as to charge Julian, he had worked all that out.

The timeline surely presented problems. Not enough problems to keep Jack from arresting Julian, though.

Ellery absently pulled on Watson's silky ears, weighing his options.

Jack had to be pretty sure of his case to risk arresting the son of one of Pirate Cove's wealthiest and most influential families.

"Please. I'm depending on you."

Julian sounded so desperate.

Ellery closed his eyes, trying not to remember that sweet kiss and Julian's disarming, *"I can't believe you're really here."*

His cell rang again. He opened his eyes. Another call from Nora. He shuddered at the idea that they would have to come up with a statement for Sue Lewis and the *Scuttlebutt Weekly*. He really did not want to get involved in this.

But.

It couldn't hurt to talk to Julian, right? He could hear him out and then decide what, if anything, he could do.

Coffee helped.

Two aspirin, a shower, and breakfast helped more.

While he finished his second cup of coffee, Ellery tried returning the unknown number in his messages and got Buck Island City Jail. Uh-oh. He hung up and phoned Jack at the familiar PICO PD number.

It took a few tries, but eventually Jack picked up. He sounded weary but unsurprised. "What did you need, Ellery? I don't have a lot of time to talk."

Ellery was equally short. "No problem. You're not the one I want to talk to."

Jack sighed. "The answer is no. You can't speak to Julian."

"Why can't I?"

Jack spluttered, "What do you mean, why? Because he's not staying in a hotel. He's in jail. For homicide."

"He's allowed a phone call, isn't he?"

"Of course."

"Well, he used it to call me."

"He phoned you?"

"Yes. Three times."

There was a silence, and then Jack said, "I see."

Judging by his tone, he did see something. Something that Ellery did not. And that Jack, being Jack, was not going to share.

Ellery lost patience. "Come on, Jack. What does it hurt if I speak to him for a minute? What do you think I'm going to tell him? What do you think he's going to tell me?"

Jack gave a funny laugh. "I'm sure I'll find out soon enough."

"Then I can talk to Julian?"

"Yes. You can talk to Julian."

Before Ellery could respond, Jack put him on hold. Ellery waited through several public-service announcements. Then there were a couple of *clicks*, the phone rang, there was another *click*, and Julian said tentatively, "Hello?"

"Hi. It's me. Ellery."

Julian exhaled in a long, unsteady sigh. "Thank God. I knew you'd call. Ellery, I didn't do it. I swear to God. I didn't kill Brett."

"I know," Ellery said automatically. "Of course not."

"I'm not sorry he's dead. I'm not going to pretend I am."

It suddenly occurred to Ellery what Jack's I'm-sure-I'll-find-out-soon-enough comment had meant. Julian's phone calls were being recorded. That wasn't the surprise. The surprise was that Jack had hinted as much to Ellery. Did he *want* Ellery to know he was being recorded?

Why?

"Sure, but I wouldn't stress that, if I were you," Ellery said.

"I'm not a hypocrite. I'm not—"

Ellery cut him off. "Why were you arrested? What kind of evidence do they have against you?"

"I don't know!" Julian's voice shot up, and Ellery frowned.

"You must have some idea."

"I guess because I found the body. The person who finds the body is always the prime suspect."

"What about the scuffle with Brett earlier in the evening? What happened when you went outside? You weren't alone with him, were you?"

"No!"

"At any point after that run-in were you alone with Brett?"

Julian hesitated. "*No.* No, of course not."

Ellery's hope faded. He didn't need to know Julian well to hear the lie in his voice. That didn't mean Julian had killed Brett. People lied when they were afraid, and Julian was audibly terrified.

"Listen," he said. "I have some experience with this, and I can tell you that being honest with Jack—with Police Chief Carson—is your best bet. Even if he doesn't believe you—he didn't believe me at first when I was suspected of killing Trevor Maples—he'll keep looking until he figures out the truth."

Julian said bitterly, "Maybe that's how it worked for you, but that's not how it is now. He's acting like he hates me. He doesn't believe anything I say. He keeps asking the same stupid questions over and over, even when I tell him I don't know the answers. I don't know why I ever thought he was so hot. He's a jerk."

Ellery cleared his throat. "That's his job, though. To see if there are discrepancies in your story. To see where he can follow up."

"He's not going to follow up on anything. He thinks I did it. All this time I believed he was one of the good guys, but he's already thrown away the key."

Ellery let that go. He understood Julian's need to vent, but they didn't have a lot of time to talk. "Julian, who do *you* think killed Brett?"

Once again, Julian's voice rocketed skyward. "I don't know! How should I know?"

"Well, he's—was—married to your mother. You must have some idea of who he knew, and where he went, and why someone might not like him."

"Brett was a weasel."

"Right. But was he a-a generic weasel, or was there something weasel-specific that he did to someone that might make them want him dead?"

"I'm sure there were lots of things!"

Ellery held on to his patience. "Okay. If you had to guess who killed Brett—"

"That horrible bitch Kezzie Harwood. Obviously. *Obviously*, she's the one who did it. There isn't anyone else."

That directly contradicted what Julian had just said about lots of things Brett might have done that could make someone want to murder him. Also, as a veteran mystery reader, Julian had to know his own mother would be a prime suspect.

Although, in fairness, he might not believe that. And even if he did, he'd have to be pretty cold to throw his momma under that train.

Ellery sighed. It must have come out sounding more tired than he intended because Julian said with a little flare of panic, "You'll help me, won't you? You won't let Chief Carson make me the fall guy for this?"

"It isn't that I don't want to help. It's just that I'm not sure what I can do. I'm not... I don't..."

Arf. Arf. Arf.

Ellery rose and went to the kitchen windows to see what Watson was getting up to. No worries. Watson was chasing a very large grasshopper through the dead herb garden, barking all the way.

"You *have* to help me," Julian protested. "You're the only one I can turn to."

Oh no. This was much worse than he'd imagined. Did Julian's *mother* believe he was guilty?

Ellery faltered. "But don't you have a lawyer? Isn't your mother going to hire someone to defend you? Can't *you* hire someone to defend you?"

"Of course! My mother hired Hiram Charcuterie. They're arranging for bail now. I mean help solving this case. Help proving me innocent."

"But I'm not a detective," Ellery said. "The police—"

"*No.* I'm telling you, the police think I did it. Chief Carson believes I killed Brett." Julian's voice rose hysterically. "It *has* to be you. You *have* to help me."

"But—"

"You did it before. You solved Trevor Maples' murder, and you solved Brandon Abbott's murder. You *are* a detective."

"No, I'm really not. I've never even played one on TV."

"You're the only one I can trust!"

"Julian, you're not—"

"Please. *Please* help me."

Ellery's resolve wavered in the face of that desperation and fear.

"I-I'll try. I'm just not sure what I can do. I really don't think I'm the best person—"

"*Promise* me," Julian pleaded. "*Promise* you'll help."

All at once Ellery was also desperate. Desperate to end this call. Desperate to get off the phone. He said, knowing even as the words were spoken, that it was unwise, "All right. I promise."

CHAPTER ELEVEN

Ellery knew what it was like to be suspected of murder.

He knew how it felt to have people cross the street when they saw you coming or stop talking when you entered a shop. How it felt to have people watching and whispering and all too easily believing the worst of you.

So he got it. And Julian had his sympathy.

But he couldn't help feeling that he had been pressured into doing something he was not equipped to do. That he wasn't sure he *wanted* to do.

Jack wasn't a fool. Far from it. And if Jack thought he had enough evidence to charge Julian, he definitely had enough to charge him.

That didn't mean Jack couldn't be wrong.

Julian had seemed genuinely shocked by the discovery of Brett's body. But there was such a thing as acting, after all, and maybe that's what Julian had been doing.

Anyway, Ellery had agreed—promised, in fact—to help Julian, and a promise was a promise. He would do what he could. Maybe, at least, he could come up with some useful points for Julian's defense, on the awful chance he actually went to trial.

But first things first.

He picked up the phone to return Sue Lewis's message, considered, reconsidered, and decided he might have more luck dealing with Sue in person.

Not that he ever had so far, but there could always be a first time. He grabbed his phone, located his wallet, went to the front door, and whistled for Watson.

Sometimes Watson responded to Ellery's whistle. Sometimes he had better things to do. This morning he responded, scampering up all bright-eyed and bushy-tailed. Literally bushy-tailed. Dead brush had attached itself to his tail, and he was dragging it behind him.

Ellery detached the shrubbery.

"Wanna go for a drive?"

The answer to any question beginning with *wanna?* was always yes, in Watson's opinion, and he voiced his approval. Ellery snapped the puppy into his blue harness, found his leash, found his shoes— Ellery's shoes, not Watson's, although they did seem to share ownership, judging by the teeth marks—and bundled the puppy into the VW.

* * * * *

"I was starting to get worried!" Nora greeted Ellery when he and Watson walked through the front door of the Crow's Nest. "Such a terrible thing to have happened at your first Marauder's Masquerade."

It probably wouldn't have been much better at his second or third Marauder's Masquerade either, but Ellery didn't argue.

"I thought I'd better come in today for a few hours at least." He knelt to take Watson out of his harness. "Has Sue Lewis accused me of murder yet?"

He was partly joking, so Nora's noncommittal, "Mmm," jerked his head up.

"She didn't really accuse me, did she?"

"No. She did stress your relationship to Julian Bloodworth—"

"There isn't a relationship. I was his date. That's it." Okay, and he'd signed on to help clear Julian of murder charges, so maybe there was a relationship, come to think of it.

"And she emphasized your previous history with…law enforcement," Nora said delicately.

Ellery rose. "My previous history? You mean dating Jack?"

"No. Your *other* history with law enforcement."

"If I have a previous history, it's helping to solve the increasingly alarming caseload of murders in this village."

"Now, now. I know that. We all know that. Everyone in Pirate's Cove can read between the lines of Sue Lewis's…"

"Vendetta?"

"Editorial. I've been mulling this over all morning, and I really think our best strategy is to prepare an official statement. She'll have to run it, whether she likes it or not."

"Nope. I'm going to talk to her myself," Ellery said grimly.

Nora looked uneasy. "Dearie, I really don't think—"

"I do."

"Everyone's a little bit shocked and tired and, well, *under the weather* this morning. Wouldn't it be better to wait until you've had a chance to speak to Chief Carson? He's the best person to clarify the situation for Sue."

Ellery laughed without humor. "I already talked to Jack this morning."

"You did?"

"Yes. And Julian."

"Oh!" Nora looked impressed. "What do you think? He always seemed like such a nice boy. Highly strung, true." Her gaze was speculative. "Did he...?"

"What? Confess? No. He says he didn't do it."

"Do you believe him?"

Ellery hesitated. "I want to. I think I do."

Nora nodded thoughtfully. "I suppose that's how it was for Chief Carson when you were suspected of killing Trevor Maples."

Was it? That was a depressing thought.

"He wants me to help him. To help prove him innocent."

Nora's pale eyes blazed with delight and excitement. "That's wonderful!"

"Not exactly the word I'd have used." Ellery couldn't help smiling a little at Nora's instant and utter enthusiasm.

"But it is. You're exactly the person to solve this ghastly crime."

"Yeah, again, not how I'd put it."

"But you *are*," Nora insisted. "Look at your record."

"The very thing I'm hoping to avoid."

"With the help of the Silver Sleuths, you'll have this case wrapped up in no time."

"Uh, sure. I'm going to go speak to Sue. Will you keep an eye on Watson?"

Nora had already turned away. She waved, whether in agreement or shooing him off was unclear, and picked up the phone.

The "offices" of the *Scuttlebutt Weekly* were housed—literally—in a cozy, gray clapboard cottage at the west end of the village.

Staring at the cherry-red door, blooming flower boxes, and triangle-shaped shrubs, Ellery felt like he'd taken a wrong turn somewhere. This was all so cute and quaint. From the charming sign with its gossiping-fish masthead, the bike rack, the pristine stars and stripes snapping briskly in the sea breeze, it just did not look like a place where Sue Lewis would work. Granted, there were no maximum-security prisons on the island, so she probably had to take what she could get.

He walked up to the front door, glanced at the front page of the paper in the newspaper stand beside the walkway, and felt his blood begin to boil.

FOOL ME THREE TIMES, SHAME ON...?

Ellery banged on the cherry-red door.

"Come in," called a cheerful male voice.

Ellery opened the door onto a long room divided into cubicles. Three people sat in the cubicles, all of them staring at him with interest. Ellery knew Mia Lewis, Sue's teenaged daughter, only by sight. Lucas Roy, who wasn't a lot older than Mia, was a regular customer at the bookstore (he preferred true crime) and had started his journalistic career as a paperboy. "Cap" Elijah Murphy was a crony of Nora's from their days in Pirate's Cove Historical Society. Cap wrote a regular opinion column for the *Scuttlebutt Weekly*, which boiled down to a weekly rant about all the changes to the island that he did not approve of—which was all the changes to the island.

The interest on their three faces changed to varying degrees of alarm when they recognized Ellery.

"Ellery!" Cap exclaimed with false heartiness. "What brings you here this fine and sunny morning?"

Mia grabbed her phone, punched a button, and began to whisper frantically.

"Ellery. Hey!" Lucas glanced nervously down the length of the room at a closed door with a placard that read: SUSAN LEWIS – EDITOR IN CHIEF.

"I'd like to speak to Sue," Ellery said tersely.

Cap pointed. "Door next to the fireplace. Knock twice."

Lucas threw Cap a look of disbelief and stammered, "Is-is there anything we can help you with?"

"No." Ellery strode toward Sue's door. A large brown-and-white cat leaped from its spot in front of the cold fireplace as though a dog had suddenly appeared.

The door to Sue's office flew open. Sue stood framed in the entrance with a wary smile on her face. "Ellery. What a pleasant surprise."

"Is it?"

Sue's perfectly groomed brows arched in wonder. "Well, yes. You've turned down all my previous requests for an interview. But I suppose it's different this time. Given your relationship with the prime suspect."

"You thought wrong." Positioned as he was, Ellery could see into Sue's office. Her desk was a pile of papers, coffee cups, and Ding Dongs wrappers. On the wall behind the desk hung a calendar. The bottom half of the calendar was a series of intimidating red slashes to mark the passing days—all of which Sue had apparently hated. The top half of the calendar was a disconcertingly fetching photo of Jack in becomingly fitted black breeches. Pirate Jack was shirtless, sexy, and clearly self-conscious as he hitched a debonair black frock coat over his right shoulder.

For a split-second Ellery couldn't remember what it was he had been planning to say to Sue.

Sue took advantage of his speechlessness. "Why don't we step into my office?"

Ellery snapped back to consciousness. "I think it's better if everyone hears what I have to say. First, I'm not in a relationship with Julian Bloodworth. I met him for the first time last night. He is not my boyfriend."

"That's not what everyone says," Sue retorted. "That's not what Julian says."

"I don't care. I met him last night. End of story."

Sue opened her mouth.

"Second, I've tried to be a good sport, but you keep pushing it. I don't know what your problem with me is, Sue." Ellery couldn't help another automatic look at Pirate Jack's pained grin. "But if you don't stop, and I mean now, I'm going to sue you for libel."

Maybe Sue caught that inadvertent peek, because her smile grew tighter. "Get off your high horse, Ellery. You can barely keep the Crow's Nest afloat now. You're not suing anyone. Just be glad I don't sue *you*. For harassment."

"You forget. I inherited Brandon Abbott's literary estate."

Sue stopped smiling.

"And you know who has more money than both of us put together? The Bloodworths."

Sue's eyes went wide. She didn't seem to have a response. Had it only occurred to her then that her poison darts were hitting targets besides Ellery?

Ellery turned and headed for the door. He paused on his way out to tell their dumbstruck audience, "Just remember, the next time she does one of her hatchet jobs on me, she's putting your jobs at risk as well."

Sue recovered enough to yell, "There's something called freedom of the press, you know!"

Ellery shot back, "There's also something called defamation of character." He slammed the door shut.

Would it do any good?

Ellery had no idea, but it had *felt* good in the moment.

It wasn't until he was back in his Volkswagen, scrolling through the village directory for Klementina Harwood's address, that he realized he had never even read Sue's article. How funny and yet sad that Sue's use of the *Scuttlebutt Weekly* as a platform for venting her frustration and dislike was so predictable.

Unable to locate Kezzie in the directory, Ellery phoned Nora.

"She rents the old Montgomery place, dearie." Nora's words were neutral, but her tone was, *That woman is not one of us!*

"Where's the old Montgomery place?"

"It's the large blue house on Shell Neck Road. But don't you think it might be a good idea to wait to interview her? I've called an emergency meeting of the Silver Sleuths for this evening."

Ellery's plans for the evening included a hot bath, a good book, and his very comfortable bed. The headache he'd woken up with had only gotten worse over the course of the day, and the thought of an evening with the Silver Sleuths was not helping any.

"I might have better luck if I catch her while she's still hungover."

"Hmm. True." Nora cleared her throat. "Chief Carson stopped by a little while ago."

"Did he?"

"He seemed to think you would be working today."

"He's often wrong."

"He said something about catching up with you later."

Ellery muttered darkly, "Hmmpf."

"Of course, dearie," Nora said in the soothing tone of one who sees all too clearly. "Good luck with Ms. Harwood. Let me know how it goes."

CHAPTER TWELVE

It took several short, stubborn rings and Ellery leaning on the doorbell for a solid thirty seconds before the glass door of 1728 Shell Neck Road finally swung open.

"What the hell do you *want*?" Kezzie Harwood moaned, peering at him through slitted eyes. She held an ice pack to her head with one hand and dribbled what looked like a lime spritzer with the other.

Ellery stepped out from under the rainfall of lime spritzer. "Three minutes of your time."

"Do I *know* you?"

Good question. If he hadn't known for sure this was the right address, he might not have recognized Kezzie. She wore plum-colored capris, and was much shorter without the haystack-sized wig. Minus all the red velvet and lace, she was a waif of a woman with bruised-looking blue eyes, severely cropped black hair, and a colorless face beneath smoked-purple lipstick.

"I was at the party last night. I'm Julian's friend."

"Oh God. *Julian.*" Her face twisted. "I still can't believe it."

"Me neither." Any of it. All of it.

"Come in." She backed up, nearly overbalanced, and caught herself. "Did you want a drink?"

"Uh...sure. Whatever you're having." Ellery couldn't believe he'd gotten inside so easily. He closed the door and followed her unsteady progress down the sunlit hall.

"I wouldn't have thought he had the wherewithal." Kezzie dropped her ice pack on a small shaker table, glancing back at Ellery. "No offense, but you know what I mean."

"Well..." Ellery hedged.

"Oh, sure. I get it. And he's crazy about *you*. But I mean, who would have thought he could be *violent*?"

They had reached a bright and sunny open-concept kitchen with distressed wooden floors and a wall of windows looking out over sandy white beach. Kezzie went to the fridge and took out a bottle of sparkling water. "I don't know about you, but I'm never drinking again."

She stopped, frowning.

Uh-oh. She wonders what I'm doing here.

Kezzie brightened. "Glasses. Right." She pointed at a row of white cupboards. "Can you be a love?"

"Sure." Ellery got out a tall glass and brought it to Kezzie, who took it with shaking hands. She squeezed lime into the fizzy water. "Oh God. I forgot the ice."

"No worries," Ellery said. "I don't need ice."

"Let's sit out on the deck. I need fresh air."

Ellery followed her out through sliding glass doors to a long, weathered deck. She collapsed into a pillow-lined hammock chair and closed her eyes.

"Are you okay?" Ellery asked.

She shook her head. Opened her eyes. "What was your name again?"

"Ellery."

"Right. You're the actor. You played Jason?"

Ellery nearly did a spritzer spit-take. "No. I was in the *Happy Halloween! You're Dead* movies. It was a long time ago."

"Right?" She closed her eyes again.

Ellery wasn't sure if she had drifted off. He watched the hypnotic wash of waves over the shore, listened to the gulls squawking overhead. Between the sound of the waves, the warmth of the sun, and his own hangover, he was tempted to close his eyes too.

Kezzie said suddenly, "Marguerite, now *that* I could believe." She stared at Ellery bleakly.

"Really?"

"Sure. She did it before."

"She…"

"Seriously?" Kezzie rolled her eyes so hard, they nearly disappeared in the back of her skull. "Don't pretend you don't know."

"Well, I sort of thought…"

"She got away with it once, so she figured she could get away with it a second time. She's a cold-hearted bitch." She wiped angrily at the tears leaking down the sides of her face. "I really loved that man, you know what I mean?"

Ellery nodded, though in fact, he had no clue. Zero.

"I'm not kidding myself he was an angel. I wouldn't *want* an angel. We understood each other."

After all, the only way to play a part convincingly was to throw yourself into it. He cannonballed into the deep end. "That's how it seemed to me."

"What we had was special."

"Exactly."

"That they would arrest Julian... *Julian?* He's *harmless.* The only good part about this, is it will *kill* Marguerite that her adored Julian got caught in her web. Coldhearted..." She trailed off, staring moodily at the ocean.

Ellery said, "The thing I can't figure out is why she'd kill Brett. Why not just divorce him?"

Kezzie scowled. "That's obvious."

"Is it?"

"Of course. No one leaves Marguerite. Not Ambrose or whatever his name was. Not Julian. And sure as hell not Brett. As far as she's concerned, Brett was signed, sealed, and delivered." She put her face in her hands. "Poor Brett. Poor, poor Brett." She began to massage her temples.

Ellery rummaged around for another line of questioning. He said tentatively, "Were the police horrible to you too?"

Kezzie sat up. "Oh God! Were they horrible to you? I bet they were. I bet they're all *totally* homophobic. That tin-pot chief of police is such an arrogant jerk. Sitting there all smug and judgy. Small-town minds. All of them."

"Yeah." Ellery refrained from pointing out that Jack was from Los Angeles and had been a detective with LAPD.

"I'm sure that's part of why they decided to make Julian the scapegoat. I feel *so* sorry for you guys. But you know, Julian will probably get off on grounds of..." She whistled a two-note cuckoo call.

"Thanks," Ellery said faintly.

Okay. This was starting to get unsettling—for a variety of reasons. For one thing, he did not dislike Klementina Harwood nearly as much as he'd expected. In fact, he kind of felt sorry for her. She really did seem genuinely broken up about Brett.

For another thing, he felt like he already had more information than he knew what to do with. And if not actual information, at least troubling hints at information he suspected he was not going to like. Interviewing Kezzie was like trying to herd cats. Cute little cats with giant claws and fangs.

He finished his sparkling lime and rose. Kezzie didn't seem to notice. She continued to stare grimly at the waves hitting the sand.

"Thanks for your time."

She nodded, still not looking at him.

"Will you be all right?"

"No." She looked at him then. "You're a nice boy. Don't get involved with that family. Pirates. Incest. Madness. Murder. Steer clear. Take my word for it."

Yikes.

"Okay. Well…"

She shaded her eyes. "You won't listen. You're in love. But that bloodline is *tainted*."

"Ohhhhhh-kay," Ellery said. "Thanks again. And I'm-I'm sorry for your loss."

Kezzie turned her profile to him and went back to gazing at the sunlit water.

A mint-condition blue Buick Roadmaster Skylark was parked in the drive when Ellery walked down the front porch steps of Kezzie's beach house.

Locke Lombard, dressed in jeans and a high-end denim work shirt, was peering through the driver's window of Ellery's VW.

"Hi, Locke. Can I help you?"

Locke visibly started and straightened. "I was just—" He peered more closely. "Ellery Page?"

"Yes. How are you?"

"I didn't recognize you for a moment."

"I look different without my pantaloons."

Locke looked taken aback. "What's that? *Oh. Right. Very good.*" His smile was brief and distracted. "What are you doing here? I didn't realize you and Klementina were friends."

"Julian asked me to check on her." The fib slipped out so easily, Ellery was almost dismayed. Acting was one thing. Turning into a pathological liar was another.

"*Julian* did?"

"I spoke to him this morning."

If anything, Locke looked more confused. He glanced at the blue beach house and then back at Ellery.

"How's Marguerite?" Ellery asked.

Locke shook his head. "Not good. Julian has been denied bail."

Ellery didn't have to act. His consternation was genuine. "Oh no. But why?"

"Chief Carson managed to make a convincing case that young Julian is a flight risk."

"But…"

"Which, frankly, he is," Locke admitted. "But Marguerite would never have permitted that. She's never run from a fight in her life, and this case is very weak. It's entirely circumstantial. There's no forensic evidence to support Julian being charged, let alone convicted. I hate to say it because I've always liked Chief Carson, but I think he's in over his head."

"You do know he used to be a homicide detective with LAPD," Ellery couldn't help pointing out.

Locke looked nonplussed. "I didn't know that, no. But I stand by what I said. If it's not lack of experience, then it's sheer laziness. Julian discovered the body; therefore, Julian must be guilty. It's nonsense." Naturally, Locke did not actually say *nonsense.*

"I'm not sure what his motive is supposed to be." Ellery knew he should be asking Locke about *his* relationship with Kezzie, but he couldn't seem to think of a way to phrase it that wouldn't sound rude and totally random.

"There *isn't* a motive. Why would there be? Julian didn't like Brett. So what? None of us did. He would hardly wait ten years, or until the night of the Marauder's Masquerade, to get rid of him. And in such a bizarre and unlikely way. It's…"

"Nonsense," agreed Ellery, and he too did not really say *nonsense.*

Locke seemed to remember who he was talking to—or perhaps that he did not truly know who he was talking to. He regarded Ellery curiously. "You say Julian phoned you this morning?"

"Yes."

"Then I take it things went well last night?"

"I'm not sure our finding Julian's stepfather dead in the family mausoleum should be classified as *things went well last night.*"

"Er, no. True." Locke eyed him with uncomfortable intentness. "But you like Julian? Until the…tragedy, you were having a nice time?"

"I was having a very nice time," Ellery admitted.

"You wouldn't be here now if you didn't like him, surely?" Locke was still giving him that peculiar look.

"I guess that's true." Ellery offered his best professional smile, the bright and blank display of perfect teeth that had made Elliot Parker such a hit with teenaged girls from his very first appearance on the original *Happy Halloween! You're Dead* movie poster.

Even Locke blinked in the brightness of the light show. "I confess I'm still a little confused as to why Julian wanted you to check up on Klementina. He seemed to detest her."

"I'm not sure," Ellery said, which pretty much summed up his entire investigation.

"It's one piece of good news anyway."

Was it?

"Marguerite could use some good news today." Locke glanced again at the beach house. "How is Klementina?"

"Sad," Ellery said. "I think she maybe really loved him."

"Hard to believe, but yes. You could be right." Locke nodded politely, moving past Ellery. He turned back. "By the way, would you want to sell the bug?"

"I'm sorry?"

Locke smiled. "The beetle. Your VW. A 1950s Volkswagen Beetle in fair condition with less than one hundred thousand miles on it? I'll make you a more than fair offer. How does fifteen grand sound?"

"You're kidding," Ellery said.

"No. I collect cars. It's my passion. I can't tell you what a delight it is finding a little jewel like this one on the island.

"Little jewel" was not how Ellery would have described Great-great-great-aunt Eudora's clunker, which, showing how much he knew, he had figured was from the 1970s.

"I'll think about it for sure," Ellery said.

"Please do. I'd love to add her to my collection." Locke nodded goodbye, turned, and headed for the silent blue house.

CHAPTER THIRTEEN

"**W**ere you able to ask him what *he* was doing at Klementina Harwood's?" Nora asked.

Ellery shook his head. He said apologetically, "It's hard asking strangers personal questions."

He was back at the Crow's Nest, sharing a veggie wrap with Nora as he reported his findings.

"That's not such a personal question."

"Maybe not, but I couldn't think of a polite way to say, *Hey, what* are YOU *doing here?* How is it my business what he's doing there?" At Nora's look of exasperation, Ellery said defensively, "You know amateur sleuthing in real life is nothing like in books."

"Of course not. It's like in police work. You have to be willing to ask awkward questions."

"But I'm not the police. I don't have a right to ask anybody anything. I have to figure out ways to get them to *want* to talk to me, to *want* to offer up information."

"People are always happy to talk to a handsome and personable young man."

"Not everybody," Ellery informed her. "I don't think Locke was thrilled to see me. And I don't think he believed me when I said Julian had asked me to check on Kezzie."

"It's true, though. In a way, Julian did that very thing," Nora assured him. "He wants you to solve this case, so he wants you to talk to our suspects."

"Right."

Nora patted his hand. "You're just experiencing sophomore slump, that's all. You'll get your mojo back. Don't you worry."

Ellery had to laugh at the idea of him having some kind of sleuthing mojo. He handed a sliver of carrot to Watson, who had been watching him hopefully throughout his meal, then remembered too late he wasn't going to do that anymore.

"Klementina said something about Marguerite having committed murder before."

Nora sniffed disapprovingly.

"What's that supposed to mean?"

"Idle gossip. That's all that is."

Talk about the pot calling the kettle black. Ellery said gravely, "Okay, but what was she hinting at? Some old scandal, obviously."

"It's terrible that this would get dragged up again, but I suppose it's inevitable, given the circumstances." Nora grimaced. "Amory Bloodworth, Marguerite's first husband—Julian's father—was quite a bit older than she."

Pirates. Incest. Madness. Murder.

"Bloodworth?"

"Yes. He was a distant cousin. Very distant. As well as being nearly twenty years her senior—"

"Twenty *years!*"

Nora repeated firmly, "As well as being nearly twenty years her senior, Amory was very wealthy. By that time, the island Bloodworths had suffered a decline in fortunes, and there were those who believed that Marguerite married Amory for his money. In fact, the rumor was her father auctioned her off to the highest bidder."

"*What?*"

"It's complete nonsense," Nora comforted. "But you know how people talk."

Oh yes. Ellery did for sure know that.

"You had only to see them together to know they were deeply in love. Amory *adored* her, and he was able to provide the stability and security she'd never known. Sadly, seven years after they were married, Amory became terminally ill."

"That *is* sad."

"Yes."

Ellery said slowly, "And the rumor is Marguerite hurried him out the door and into the family mausoleum?"

"Very good." Nora smiled approvingly. "Yes. Nothing was ever proven. I don't recall there even being an official investigation. If she did have a hand in shortening Amory's suffering, it would have been out of love, not greed."

Ellery smiled. "You're a romantic, Nora."

"No, not at all." Nora seemed surprised at the idea. "But when people truly care for each other, you can see it. It shows in little ways *and* big ways."

Having spent much of his film career convincing audiences he was desperately in love with a series of very buxom and very doomed girlfriends, Ellery refrained from comment.

Nora said, "You can see how people might jump to connect dots that aren't necessarily dots."

"If they're not dots, what are they?"

"I'm sure Marguerite thought some of them were stars. The years with Brett? *Those* would have been dots."

Ellery snorted. "How *did* Marguerite wind up with Brett? Just in the little I saw of them, they didn't look like two people who belonged together."

"No. That marriage was a mistake from the first." Nora's sigh was pensive. "I imagine she finally just got tired of waking up alone and going to bed at night alone..."

Ellery remembered that Nora's husband had died a few years earlier. He wasn't quite sure what to say.

As though reading his thoughts, Nora said briskly, "However, Brett must have had some good points because Marguerite had plenty of opportunity to divorce him."

"Maybe there was a prenuptial agreement."

Nora threw him a look of surprise. "Maybe. Still, I've always thought Marguerite was a coolheaded, pragmatic woman. It's hard to believe she'd come up with such a convoluted, melodramatic means of getting rid of an unwanted spouse. Would she really shoot him with her own gun?"

Ellery stared. "Where did you hear that?"

"It came out at the bail hearing."

This was not good news. If Brett had been shot with Marguerite's gun, it was one more strike against Julian. No one would believe he hadn't had access to the weapon.

"A hard shove down the stairs, a balcony railing giving way," Nora was saying dreamily. "That's how you do it."

"Sometimes you scare me," Ellery remarked. "And speaking of things to be scared of, what did Jack have to say when he stopped by?"

Nora stopped daydreaming perfect crimes. "Not much. He said he would get hold of you later."

"He can try."

Nora neatly balled up her sandwich wrapper. "Poor Chief Carson. He looked so tired. I think this case is weighing on him. And, as if he didn't have enough on his plate with another homicide, there were *two* burglaries last night."

"Two? You're not serious."

"I'm afraid I am. These thieves are growing more brazen by the day. Both the Lyman and Dunmore houses were hit. Chief Carson said the thieves made off with quite a haul because Mrs. Lyman had left her jewelry case out on her nightstand."

"When you think about it, with half the island gathered at the Marauder's Masquerade, last night was the perfect setup."

"Yes. Exactly. And there are people who blame Chief Carson for not anticipating that."

Ellery said indignantly, "What's Jack supposed to do? He can't post an officer at every house on the island, even if he did have more than a handful of officers. It's not his fault so many of these vacation houses don't have security systems. Heck, most of them don't even have decent window locks."

His own included.

Nora's sigh was mournful. "True. But he's taking it very much to heart. I've never seen shadows beneath his eyes like I did today."

Ellery tilted his head, studied Nora. "Now you're laying it on too thick."

She lifted a shoulder in acknowledgment. "He *is* worried, though. I can tell."

"That I believe." Jack was nothing if not conscientious.

"He could use a friend."

Ellery scowled. "He has a friend. And he knows it. So can we stop talking about Jack?"

"Of course, dearie. After all, you're the one who brought up—" She stopped at Ellery's look.

The bell on the front door chimed in welcome as two middle-aged men carrying what were clearly their wives' shopping bags came in. Nora rose to greet them, asking about their trip on the ferry and deftly determining their reading preferences.

Ellery listened absently. His headache, which had faded earlier, was back with a vengeance. And no wonder, considering everything he'd learned over lunch, particularly the very bad news that the gun used to kill Brett had come from the Bloodworth house. Locke Lombard had been right. The case against Julian was almost entirely circumstantial, but the circumstances were piling up fast.

When the customers had departed with their purchases, he joined Nora at the counter.

"If you're okay here on your own, I think I'm going to head home and get some sleep. I'm still feeling a little…"

"Seedy?" Nora supplied. "Drunkover?

"I was going to say under the weather."

"Don't you worry." Nora beamed at him. "Everything is under control here. Tonight the Silver Sleuths will meet and go over what you've learned today. There's plenty to sift through. And tomorrow we can start fresh. This crime is all but solved."

"Are you being ironic?"

Nora winked. "Have a nice, quiet evening, dearie."

A nice, quiet evening was exactly what Ellery had in mind.

That didn't mean he couldn't do a little research as well. Great-great-great-aunt Eudora's warehouse of miscellaneous books, i.e., her "library," had turned out to be a treasure trove for research.

Ellery suspected his eccentric relation had collected every book ever written about Buck Island. There was also an alarming number of tomes on malaria and lost treasure, so maybe it wasn't fair to blame the peculiar diversity in literature all on Great-great-great-aunt Eudora. The library had predated her just as it predated Ellery. It did make him wonder about the relatives on his father's side of the family.

Anyway, once he was home and had taken Watson for a cobweb-clearing walk in the meadow, he drew himself a bath in the insanely oversize claw-foot tub, dug out a battered copy of 1955's *Historic and Architectural Resources of Buck Island, Rhode Island* by Philby Hammond, Esq., and settled down for a relaxing soak and a read.

He was amused by the author's description of Buck Island as "a trip back in time," and lamentations over "the incursion of modern life" with the replacement of power-line poles along Castle Road, and he was fascinated—and distracted—by the black-and-white photos of Then and Now, with Hammond's Now being Ellery's Then.

It took a while to find what he was looking for, but at last he had it.

The island cemetery is next on the left. Tread cautiously upon the hallowed ground of spirits and gravestones, for here lie in eternal peace the forbearers of those present residents who consider themselves natives. Fame, fortune, and tragedy can be read between the lines of these brief and sentimental epitaphs. Overlooking this peaceful glade stands a marble mansion of the dead: the private mausoleum built by the notorious "Gentleman Pirate" Tom Blood. Though construction was completed four years before Thomas Bloodworth's death, none were laid to rest in that gilded tomb until the death of Clarence Bloodworth in 1903.

"Ah-ha," Ellery murmured, and Watson, gnawing on a pig's knucklebone, thumped his tail in an I'm-listening.

That answered one question. There were still a daunting number left.

Ellery set the book aside and exited the bath, listening to the old plumbing gurgle and guzzle as he wrapped himself in his favorite hooded modal robe patterned with retro surfboards.

He was in the kitchen, reheating the last of Nora's tuna casserole, when he heard the doorbell ring. His heart gave an annoying jump.

He didn't get a lot of visitors. His most frequent visitor was Jack. That seemed pretty unlikely given current events, but Watson's tipped ears went up like a pair of antennae, and he sprang out of the room and down the hall.

CHAPTER FOURTEEN

"**N**ow what," Ellery growled. The growl was because his instinctive reaction was pleasure, and that was the wrong response. Jack would not be there for a social call. Jack would be there to read him the riot act.

Reluctantly, he followed the sound of the doorbell to the entry hall, where Watson was whining and whimpering, leaping up and down like a circus dog.

"Traitor."

Watson ignored him, jumping still higher.

Ellery unlocked the door, opened it, and sure enough, there was Jack, darkening his doorstep. Over the last months, his skin had turned a summery bronze, and between the suntan and his navy uniform, Jack's eyes looked intensely blue.

"Hey," Ellery said curtly.

Jack began, "He—" and then looked nonplussed. "Were you in bed?"

"No. It's five o'clock. I just had a bath." The front of his robe was gapping. He tied the belt tighter. He was definitely not dressed for receiving.

Jack's nod was crisp. "Can I come in? I'd like a word."

That was uncharacteristically formal, and Ellery felt himself tensing up, but remembered that this was Jack. The same Jack who had not so long ago saved his life—not to mention helped him change out the decrepit toilet in the downstairs powder room.

"Of course." He stepped back, and Watson shot through the open door, greeting Jack like he had returned from the wars.

Ellery's exasperation mounted. "Watson, get down." He bent to scoop up Watson, but so did Jack, and they narrowly missed colliding heads.

"Ooof," said Jack, ducking left.

"Yeesh," said Ellery, ducking right.

They gazed at each other with consternation as Watson wriggled frantically to get to Jack.

"*Really*, Watson?" Ellery demanded and handed the squirming pup to Jack. "Here. Puppygram."

"How're you doing, you rascal?" Jack tried to speak around Watson licking his chin. It was difficult to preserve a professional demeanor with a puppy trying to kiss you, but Jack did his best.

Ellery sighed. It was disarming. No use pretending it wasn't.

"I want to talk to you about Julian," Jack began.

"I know. And I know what you're going to say, Jack."

"I should hope so. I've said it often enough." But Jack didn't sound angry. He sounded...resigned. His expression was harder to read, complicated by the fact that his gaze kept dropping to the V of the lower half of Ellery's robe.

"He asked for my help," Ellery said, yanking at the flap of his robe.

"I understand that."

"He's desperate. He thinks you've already got your mind made up."

"I understand that too."

Of course he understood. Because calls into the jail were recorded and he had listened to the conversation between Ellery and Julian. Which meant he knew Ellery hadn't wanted to get involved, didn't think he was the right person to help Julian, hadn't felt he had a choice.

"I can't just..."

What? Abandon Julian to his fate? What if he *was* guilty? Nothing Ellery had discovered so far cleared Julian. Maybe even the opposite.

"I just want you to hear me out," Jack said. "I'm asking you to keep an open mind, that's all."

"If that's all, then okay."

"This isn't about you playing amateur sleuth." Jack seemed to pick his words with care. "That is, yes, it is. But you already know what I think about that."

Ellery opened his mouth, and Jack said, "And as far as the burglary at the Barbys', I'm sorry I couldn't let you out of the icehouse immediately. I was angry, yes, but the delay was really about my having to make sure the crime scene was clear. I got the idea I could use the situation to discourage you from any more sleuthing." He added ruefully, "It was a bad impulse."

Ellery was too surprised to answer. But in a way it made more sense than the notion that Jack would leave him freezing his tail off in a spider-infested ruin. Jack wasn't mean or petty. Ellery nodded slowly.

"Apology accepted?"

"Apology accepted."

Jack put Watson down, and Ellery wondered if he was stalling for time.

When Jack straightened, he was sure he was right. Jack looked uncharacteristically self-conscious. "You're very...kindhearted," he said. "I think your instinct to help can get you into trouble, and I'm afraid it's going to get you into trouble with Julian."

"I don't think I'm abnormally kindhearted," Ellery objected.

"I didn't say abnormally, but you're kind and you're loyal."

"Great. I sound like a collie."

Jack grinned faintly. "I like those things about you. But in this case, I think—I'm afraid—you're going to get hurt. That's my concern. *You* are my concern."

Jack's substitution of *think* for *afraid* held Ellery silent. Jack was so serious. His eyes were dark with… yes, concern.

"Thank you. I think. But even so, I can't—"

"I know you think I'm being unfair to Julian."

"I don't know if you're being unfair or not," Ellery admitted. "I don't know for sure that Julian didn't kill Brett. I can't see why he would. I don't *think* he did. He seemed genuinely shocked when we found Brett's body. But I don't know. I feel like it won't hurt to have another pair of eyes look at everything, and if it seems to me that he's innocent, maybe I can come up with something that will help."

Jack let out a long breath and seemed to relax. "Okay. That's kind of a relief."

"It is?"

"It's a relief that you're keeping an open mind. That you understand Julian may have committed murder."

"I *don't* think he did. But yes, I accept that it's possible."

Jack said, "I've known Julian for five years. I like him. You probably don't believe that. He doesn't believe it. But one of the first calls I caught after I got the job of police chief was to the Bloodworths'. Julian had locked himself in the bathroom and was threatening to cut his wrists."

Ellery swallowed. He could think of nothing to say.

"On another occasion, he swam out to Buccaneer's Bay and tried to drown himself."

"*Why?*"

"Both times had to do with relationships that didn't end well."

"But..."

"After the second time, Marguerite accepted that Julian's problems weren't going to be solved by fatherly chats with me."

Ellery couldn't help objecting, "You're not old enough to be his father."

"True—and that was starting to look like another problem. Marguerite faced facts and got Julian help. And as far as I know, the situation improved. However."

However.

Now things were starting to make sense.

Ellery said, "You think because he went through a-a rough patch a few years ago, he might have killed Brett."

"I think he may be emotionally unstable, yes. And I know for a fact he hated Brett. Julian frequently expressed to me his wish to have Brett out of his mother's life—and his. He once asked—jokingly—if I would be willing to kill Brett for one hundred thousand dollars."

"Jokingly, you said," Ellery protested, but no question, he was shocked.

"Joking-not-joking." Jack's expression was grim. "I have zero doubt he hoped I'd take him up on the invitation."

Ellery said slowly, "That's why you weren't happy about me going to the Marauder's Masquerade. You thought my invitation had to do with Julian."

Jack nodded. "I was sure it did."

"And you thought..."

"I thought you would show up looking like a prince walking out of the pages of a fairy tale, which is exactly what happened." Jack's tone was unexpectedly harsh. "I thought Julian would take one look at you and it would be déjà vu. Only this time you would be at the center of it. And I didn't want that. For your sake."

"I didn't realize."

"No. How could you? Which is why I'm sharing this information. Because you're my friend and I...care about you. I can't stop you from getting involved, but you have to at least understand what the risks are."

"Yes. Okay." Ellery added a belated, "Thank you."

"I'm not saying this out of jealousy," Jack added, which was such an out-of-the-blue comment. It had never occurred to Ellery that Jack was motivated by jealousy.

"I know. I didn't think you were."

Jack gave him a funny look, started to speak, stopped himself.

Ellery was trying to process everything Jack had told him. It was a lot to take in. He said, "I appreciate the honesty. I promised to try to help Julian, and I still want to. I'm just not sure how best to do that."

"I understand." Jack hesitated. "If I can help you, I will."

Ellery laughed.

"I mean it," Jack insisted. "I don't have any desire to see Julian punished for something he didn't do—or even something he didn't mean to do. If you need help, ask me, and I'll do what I can."

Jack's steady gaze held his own. Ellery said, "All right. I will."

Jack nodded. "Then I guess that's it. That's all I wanted to say."

"I'm glad you told me what was going on. I didn't think it was like you to make a snap judgment."

"Part of why I want Julian held is to make sure he doesn't panic and flee—or harm himself."

"Understood."

They continued to gaze at each other. Watson sat between them, tongue lolling as he waited for something fun to happen.

Nothing fun happened.

"Right. Well." Jack let out a breath that was a half-laugh and said, "That's a very nice robe, by the way. I like the surfboards."

Ellery answered with the shaka sign.

Jack looked quizzical. "You've never surfed, have you?"

"No." Ellery chuckled at the idea. He thought of that oft-postponed diving lesson. He suspected the chances of that date-that-would-not-really-have-been-a-date with Jack were now as far removed as him ever going surfing.

"I guess…" Jack seemed to gather himself. He said briskly, "Anyway. I appreciate your hearing me out."

"Yeah, of course. I appreciate your telling me what's really going on."

"Have a nice evening."

"I will," Ellery said. "You too. And thank you again."

He watched Jack walk out to his police SUV. Watched him climb in and drive away. Watched until the SUV's taillights vanished in the twilight and only the fireflies were left, flickering and floating over the meadow.

CHAPTER FIFTEEN

"The real mystery," Nora said, "is why no one knocked Brett Ainsley off years ago."

Ellery murmured acknowledgment, scanning the printouts and scribbled notes on legal paper in the manila folder Nora had given him when he walked in the door.

It was Monday morning at the Crow's Nest, and Nora had taken advantage of the lack of customers to present him with an unnervingly detailed, if informal, dossier compiled by the Silver Sleuths on their victim.

He swallowed a mouthful of coffee. "He must have had some good qualities. No one is all good or all bad."

"Evil is real, dearie. Don't you ever doubt it."

"Even so." Ellery remembered Brett at the masquerade, plastered and lewd and then lashing out. Not a happy guy. But there had also been the Brett who jumped to attention when Marguerite simply gave him a look."

"He is—was—very handsome," Nora admitted.

"What did he do for a living?"

Nora said tartly, "He married a wealthy woman."

"What about before he married Marguerite?" Ellery glanced at the file.

"He was a big wheel in finance. That's how they met. Mr. Lombard introduced them. But there was some sort of scandal and Brett had to be bailed out—financially. I don't know that charges were ever filed."

"What does that mean? Embezzlement? Stock manipulation? Robbing the petty cash?"

Nora shrugged. "After that, his full-time job was being Marguerite's escort."

A career as arm candy would not be easy on a man's pride. It would not be easy on anyone's pride.

Ellery tried to decipher another paragraph of scrawled handwriting on legal paper. "How did you guys find out that Brett had two DUIs?"

Nora chirped, "The DUIs are a matter of public record. As for the forged checks, charges were never brought, but Detective Lansing's wife is Maggie McGillicuddy's niece, and Maggie is Herm—"

Ellery put a hand up. "Don't tell me. If I don't know, I don't have to tell Jack he's got a mole in his department."

"A mole!" Nora chortled at the very idea. "Paying attention to volunteered information is hardly the same as spying."

"It is the way you guys do it!"

Nora preened as though Ellery were tossing bouquets at her feet. "Unfortunately, the most interesting and possibly relevant information is the hardest to verify."

"I bet."

"But it isn't as though Brett made much of an effort to hide the affair with Klementina Harwood."

Ellery had a mental image of Klementina half falling out of both her dress and Brett's lap at the Marauder's Masquerade. "True." Discretion did not seem to have been one of Brett's virtues. And judging by the notes before him, *virtue* was not one of Brett's virtues either.

"And that's been going on for some time. At least a year. Which must be a record for Brett. And then before that, there was the Mr. April situation."

Ellery grinned. "Do tell."

"Brett has been Mr. April in the Pirate's Cove calendar for the last six years. However, last year he and our then-photographer Nova Glassbottom were discovered in her studio, filming themselves performing pornographic acts."

The usually unflappable Nora sounded so indignant, it was all Ellery could do to keep a straight face. He managed a relatively steady, "No way was her name really Glassbottom."

"It certainly was!"

Nora met his eyes, made a sound very close to a giggle, but said, "It really wasn't funny, though. The calendar was almost canceled, and it's our biggest fund-raising event of the year."

"Gotcha." He finished his coffee as he continued reading through the results of some very diligent Googling.

"It's hard to imagine someone like Marguerite Bloodworth putting up with any of this," he said thoughtfully.

"That's been a puzzle to all of us for years," Nora agreed. Her expression altered. She said slowly, "There was one incident early in their marriage…"

"Incident or rumor?" Ellery asked.

"Rumor. But from a very reliable source."

"Naturally."

"Maggie McGillicuddy's third cousin, Gail, used to work as a cook at the Bloodworths'. This was several years ago. She's since passed."

Ellery said, "I think I just figured out who the Hive Queen is."

"Pshaw." Nora brushed that off. "Gail once told Maggie that the first time Marguerite caught Brett *in flagrante delicto*, she threatened to kill him."

Something about the way Nora's New Englander vowels wrapped around *in flagrante delicto* sounded disconcertingly pornographic. Ellery forced himself to concentrate.

"Yeah, but people say that all the time. I've said it myself. *If I'm late to this audition, I'm going to kill you.*" No lie, he'd probably "threatened" Todd's life over a dozen times during the course of their relationship. Todd had taken it about as seriously as Ellery had meant it, which was not at all.

"Yes. But this wasn't like that. According to Gail, Marguerite was holding Tom Blood's own dagger at the time." Nora sighed. "Granted, they were newlyweds."

"Uh…" Because nothing said marital bliss like attempted homicide? "This story sounds pretty shaky, Nora. First of all, if Gail was the cook, how would she see all this? Who goes down to the kitchen to scream at each other in front of the servants?"

"Now that, I can't say."

"It sounds to me like someone making up stories."

"Perhaps." Nora sounded a little huffy.

"I'm not questioning your sources—well, yes, I guess I am—but I think this is the kind of information we have to view skeptically, because how serious of a threat can it have been if it took Marguerite this long to get around to killing him?"

"True."

"Why not just divorce him?"

"But you could say that about any number of murders between marrieds."

Also true.

Ellery considered another angle. "You know, it would have been hard enough for Julian to get down to the graveyard and back in time. Marguerite was wearing a complicated costume. The gown alone… it had a super tight bodice and huge skirt. No way did she hoof it down to the cemetery in that dress and then raced back to the house. And if she took the gown off in order to run down there, it would probably take her twenty minutes to get the thing back on again. It's not like she could ask someone to zip her up." Costume changes were something Ellery had some experience with.

"That's a good point," Nora said. "Which is unfortunate because I do feel Marguerite has the temperament for the successful planning and execution of a murder. Whereas Julian has always struck me as passionate but rather disorganized."

Ellery's eyebrows shot up at that one. "Sure, but Marguerite never had a hair out of place all evening, and however suited she is to a career as an assassin, she'd still probably end up with smudged mascara. At the least."

Nora acknowledged this regretfully. Further discussion was postponed as the front door bell's silvery welcome rang out.

"Ho, *ho*!" Dylan pointed gleefully at Ellery. "I thought you didn't like confrontation?"

"Who me? I don't." Ellery was momentarily confused.

"What do you call your run-in with Sue Lewis yesterday morning?"

With everything that happened, Ellery had all but forgotten his showdown with Sue at the *Scuttlebutt Weekly*'s office. Truthfully, it was probably the least significant event of the day.

"There wasn't any big confrontation. I just reminded her there are libel laws."

Nora cleared her throat. "I wish you hadn't done that in front of so many witnesses, dearie. People have long memories in this village."

Ellery stared at her. "What does that mean?"

"Just that Sue is making herself so unpleasant lately. And if something *were* to happen to her, I'm afraid your name would be right at the top of the list of possible suspects."

Ellery and Dylan exchanged alarmed looks.

"Why would something happen to her?" Ellery asked.

"That's not what I meant," Dylan said quickly.

"No," Nora agreed. "It's just that one can't be too careful, and we've had a surprising number of murders in the last few months."

"True." Dylan directed another uneasy look at Nora, then turned to Ellery. "Anyway, I was going to say good for you. I don't know what's got into Sue, but hopefully this will bring her back to earth."

Ellery wasn't betting money on it. He changed the subject. "Speaking of mysterious behavior. Where've *you* been? What happened to you Saturday night?"

Dylan looked both smug and self-conscious. "Sorry for bailing on you, given all that happened after I left, but you remember September?"

"September? I wasn't here in September."

"No, no. The girl—woman—I met on Saturday. At the bar."

"Oh, right. The one who wants to be an actress."

"She *is* an actress," Dylan assured him. "She wants to join the Scallywags, and I think it's a *wonderful* idea."

Nora sniffed. Ellery avoided her gaze.

"The more the merrier."

Dylan beamed. "Exactly! This will bring new blood to the theater."

"The way things are going, I hope not."

Dylan laughed more loudly than that deserved. He did seem in very high spirits, and that was great. Who didn't want to see their friends happy and excited about a new relationship? But Ellery couldn't help saying, "I thought you and Janet were sort of..."

Dylan looked uncomfortable. "Oh, no. No. Janet is a dear friend. I *love* Janet."

"Right. Okay."

"This girl—woman. September..." Dylan kissed the tips of his fingers.

Sugar and spice and everything nice? Personally, Ellery felt that Janet, who owned Old Salt Stationery, was a good match for Dylan, but maybe they knew each other a little *too* well. Besides, Dylan was not the settling-down kind, as Miss September would soon discover.

"So that's where you were all weekend? With September?"

"Yep. She was showing me her clippings." Dylan winked.

"Yikes."

Dylan laughed heartily. "Anyway, sorry I wasn't there to stop you from tripping over another murder. I just popped in to make sure you're coming tonight."

Monday nights were game night in Pirate's Cove. Ellery had recently become a member of the Monday Night Scrabblers, where he was vying with Janet for the title of Scrabble Champion (not that there was really such a title).

"I'll be there," Ellery assured him. He enjoyed hanging out and drinking with the Scrabblers, plus they provided a great alternative source of village gossip.

"Perfect. See you then!" Dylan nodded to Nora and departed.

The doorbell chimed cheerily behind him.

"Oh dear," Nora said, pretty much echoing Ellery's feelings.

It was a slow day for sleuthing and a slower day for selling books.

During the morning, Ellery tried phoning Julian but was told he was with his lawyer. After lunch, he tried again and was told Julian was unavailable. He had no idea what that meant, but in a way, it was a relief. Jack's revelations the evening before had shaken him, no question. But just because someone had experienced emotional difficulties in the past didn't mean they were emotionally unstable forever.

He still had every intention of helping Julian, but he was less and less sure of the best way to do that. Certainly, knowing the truth about what happened to Brett was the best, really the *only*, possible starting point. If, in his poking around, he came to the conclusion that Julian *was* guilty... Well, he would have to jump off that bridge when he came to it.

Some of the objections he had raised to Nora's efforts to pin the murder on Marguerite held true for Julian as well. Julian's costume, while more conducive to running and fighting and shooting, had shown no obvious sign of strenuous use. No rips, no tears, no blood spatter—and with a victim who had been shot several times, there would have been at least *some* blood spatter.

Also, Julian's hands must have been tested for gunshot residue. The fact that Mrs. McGillicuddy's informant hadn't mentioned that tidbit surely meant the tests had proved negative? If there had been blood on Julian's clothes or residue on his hands, Ellery was pretty sure Jack would have said so when he was making his case last night.

"If you need help, ask me, and I'll do what I can."

Jack had been sincere in his offer, but Ellery didn't want to abuse that generous impulse. He figured he would hold off until he had a whole list of questions, and then hit Jack with all of them at once. That would teach him.

* * * * *

Libby was not at game night, and Tom Tulley was not happy about it.

Ellery had been about five minutes late arriving at Dylan's. He could tell by the golf carts and cars parked along the street that everyone else had already arrived, but when he walked through the front door, not a board game was in sight and the Monday Night Scrabblers were grouped in Dylan's retro modern living room, listening to Tom vent.

"I don't think I'm overbearing," Tom was saying. "Do *you* think I'm overbearing?"

By what seemed to be unanimous consent, the Monday Night Scrabblers did not think Tom was overbearing.

"Here you are!" Dylan exclaimed, coming to meet Ellery.

"Sorry I'm late—" Ellery didn't have a chance to complete his greeting before Dylan hustled him off to the bar area with its captivating display of vintage movie posters.

"What'll you have? A Tipsy Mermaid? A Drunken Pirate?"

"Tipsy Mermaid. What's going on?" Ellery threw a look back at the living room, where the low-voiced conversation continued.

"Libby has broken up with Felix." Dylan grabbed a bottle of Blue Curacao and began pouring.

"That's a shame, but they're both pretty young. They've got plenty of time to—"

"*And* she informed Tom this evening she's not going to college in the fall."

Now that was a shocker. "Why?"

"He couldn't get a clear answer out of her. Something about wanting to live life to the fullest and not waste her best years in school."

"Her best years? Isn't she nineteen?"

Dylan nodded.

"How much living life to the fullest does she think she can do in her own backyard? She lives on a tiny island with less population than most small towns. She was going to go to school in Providence. She was going to Brown. She even has a couple of grants, doesn't she?"

Dylan said darkly, "Tom thinks there's a boy involved. *Another* boy."

"Another— Oh. *Oh.*" Ellery remembered walking out of the Salty Dog with Jack the week before, and Jack's exchange of words with the spiky-haired kid with defiant eyes and ripped jeans. Ned something.

"Some young hooligan has been hanging around her. Tom has banned him from the pub."

"Is he underage?"

"No. That's the problem. He's twenty-three."

Right. Come to think of it, Jack had mentioned that. Dylan made it sound like Ned was forty and married, but Ellery got it. Libby was the darling of the Scallywags, the Monday Night Scrabblers, and the Salty Dog's regulars—which was half the island. Ned was…not.

Ellery said, "I understand where Tom is coming from, but turning this into *Romeo and Juliet* will definitely not help." Tom struck him as an overprotective dad, but maybe that was the correct response. He had no clue.

"*I* know that, and *you* know that, but she's Tom's world. And this kid has had some run-ins with the law."

"Serious run-ins, or joyriding in a golf cart?"

"Who knows?"

What had Jack said about that? A lot had happened since that night. Ellery had the impression Jack thought the kid was mostly harmless. Although he'd mentioned Ned was on his list of potential burglary suspects. That seemed unlikely to Ellery after his encounter at the Barbys'.

That job had not been pulled off by a couple of bored teenagers trying their hand at recreational B&E. These thieves had taken their time, they had made trips back and forth, they had known what they were looking for and where to find it. They had known the owners were away and that there was no security system. That operation had been well-planned and organized right down to the perps never speaking and wearing dark clothes and ski masks. Ellery was no expert, but the efficient way the thieves had dealt with his unwelcome presence seemed to rule out your typical kids behaving badly.

Granted, Ned was not a teenager, even if he looked like one.

Dylan finished with the ice shaker and poured the strained indigo liquid into a martini glass. He handed the glass to Ellery. "Cheers."

"Cheers." Ellery sipped his drink. Sweet and zingy. Nothing not to love about flavored vodka and citrus liqueur.

Dylan led the way back to the living room, where they found the emergency meeting had ended and a game board was being set up.

"What exactly did you say to Sue Lewis?" Janet asked Ellery. "Reading this morning's paper, I'd never have known you were ever at the Marauder's Masquerade. In fact, I'd never have known you were a resident of Pirate's Cove."

"Good," Ellery replied, and the others laughed.

"Sue said she's done with giving him free publicity," said Sandy, and there was more laughter.

"That kind of publicity I can do without."

"It's sad about Julian, though," Greta said. She owned the gourmet grocery store on Mizzen Street and was the one member of the Monday Night Scrabblers Ellery still felt he really didn't know at all.

"I always thought there was something off about that lad," Tom muttered.

"You wouldn't want Libby marrying into the Bloodworth money?" Janet teased.

"I would not." Tom glanced at Ellery, said dryly, "Anyway, I think his tastes run in another direction."

"But speaking hypothetically?" Janet asked.

"There's nothing hypothetical about murder."

It was a little disheartening to see how over-whelmingly public opinion was against Julian. Ellery said, "Then you all believe Julian's guilty?"

"Police Chief Carson arrested him." Sandy sounded apologetic, no doubt remembering that Ellery had been Julian's date that fateful night.

"What a load of nonsense!" Mr. Starling ex-claimed—and for the record, he did actually say *non-sense*. "That boy no more killed Brett Ainsley than I did."

"I knew it!" Janet's eyes gleamed. "You think Marguerite did it. I do too!"

"You know, I had the same idea," Greta said.

Dylan, who had gone into the dining room to set up the table for the Scrabble players, poked his head in. "Janet, Ellery, Stan, we're good to go in here. Anyone need another drink before I sit down?"

Mr. Starling ignored Dylan's call to action. He glared at Janet and Greta. "No, that is *not* what I mean. Marguerite Bloodworth would hardly stand by and see her son jailed for murder. It's perfectly obvi-ous who the real culprit is!"

"Who?" they all chorused.

Mr. Starling spluttered, "*W-w-who?* That so-called financial adviser. Locke Lombard, of course!"

CHAPTER SIXTEEN

Twelve points according to Collins Scrabble Words. Not that it mattered. The Monday Night Scrabblers had given Collins the heave-ho back in 2015, after the heinous discovery that OK was not considered a valid word. OK had been validated in 2019, but the MNS were slow to forgive.

Take for example Mr. Starling who, twenty minutes after his startling accusation against Locke Lombard, was still trying to make his case.

"He's been in love with Marguerite forever," he was saying. "You'll notice he's never married."

"Dylan isn't married," Janet pointed out. "Ellery isn't married. There are reasons for not marrying that don't have to do with lost love." She was the only one really engaging at this point. Ellery had lost interest once he'd understood that Mr. Starling had received some bad investment advice from Locke twenty years ago, and he'd never quite trusted him since.

Underpass...

"That's different," Mr. Starling said. "Dylan is a consigned bachelor, and Ellery is a kid." He'd had a couple of drinks by then. They all had. (That was kind of the point of adult game night.)

"*Confirmed* bachelor," Dylan corrected absently. He was checking cellphone messages.

"Kid!" Ellery repeated.

"You're all kids to me," Mr. Starling grumbled. "Look at the facts."

"So far you haven't presented any," Janet replied.

"Lombard's in love with Marguerite. Ainsley stands in his way. All right. It would be one thing if Ainsley were the right sort of person, but he's not. He's a...a...rotter, as we used to say in my day."

Dylan looked up at that. "Stan, you're seventy-four. No one was saying *rotter* back in 1947. Not in this country. You need to lay off the Agatha Christie."

Mr. Starling ignored him. "Ainsley humiliates Marguerite at every turn. He's rude, crude, and lewd. He sleeps with her friends. He borrows money from their neighbors. He's cruel to her only child."

"Is that true?" Ellery broke in.

"Well... He's not nice to him, let's put it that way. He's not the father figure Marguerite was hoping for."

"I doubt Marguerite was looking for a father figure." Janet grinned at Ellery, which was a first. Maybe Janet was finally starting to warm up to him?

"You know what I mean. He's no good." Mr. Starling glowered at Dylan, who was back to checking his phone. "We say *that* in this country."

"Yes, we do."

Mr. Starling turned to Ellery. "And he disappeared during the crucial minutes, didn't he?"

Ellery had to think back to when Brett had been rushed outside after the confrontation with Kezzie. Julian had gone outside, for sure. And... Yes, Locke had also gone out. But so had a bunch of others.

"How would you know that?" Dylan asked Mr. Starling. "You weren't there."

"I have my sources," Mr. Starling said loftily. "I know for a fact that Julian, Lombard, and Marguerite were *all* absent from the ball during the time in question."

Did they even know the time in question?

"Maybe they did it together," Janet joked.

"*Murder on the Orient Express...*" Ellery said slowly.

"No, no." Mr. Starling was impatient. "This wasn't a lynch mob. Locke Lombard is the sole guilty party. He's the only one with anything to gain."

"Maybe Brett's murder wasn't about gain," Ellery said. "Maybe it was a crime of passion."

"Then Lombard is still our man!" Mr. Starling placed his last tile on the board with a decisive *click*. "Ha! TUNNELS." He glanced triumphantly at the little stacks of tiles before Ellery, Janet, and Dylan.

"And I believe once the tally is complete, you'll see that I win."

Mr. Starling had indeed won that game of Scrabble.

Ellery regretfully passed on playing another round, told everyone good night—assured them that no, he did not have a hot date—and drove over to Sandy's to pick up Watson from his puppysitter.

He couldn't help feeling that between TUN-NELS and UNDERPASS, the cosmos—or maybe just the Scrabble gods—were trying to tell him something.

Nothing that he hadn't already been considering.

Nora had said that Blood was the one who had originally devised the now abandoned network of tunnels beneath the village. Given that fact, and the fact that all the original Pirate's Eight homes seemed to feature secret passages or hidden rooms, it didn't seem a stretch that Blood might have built a tunnel leading from his fortress to the sheltered cove where his ship lay anchored. Ellery's theory perhaps also explained why the first generations of Bloodworths were buried in the cemetery below and not up there in the family crypt—because the mausoleum had not been built to house the dead; it had been built to conceal the comings and the goings of the living.

Granted, it was just a theory.

"Wanna go on a little adventure?" he asked Watson.

Watson was curled into a ball in the passenger seat. Ellery could see the whites of his eyes, and heard the swish of his tail against the VW's door.

"Yeah? Me too."

Ellery turned left and wound through the village, passing Victorian cottages with friendly lights gleaming behind lacy curtains, boxy beach bungalows with summer visitors crowding their porches, until he turned onto the narrow road leading to the old cemetery.

It was not a long drive, but it was a dark and lonely one. There were very few reasons for Pirate Cove's residents to make this trek.

It was also a bumpy drive—the road did not seem to be maintained, and the VW hit a few neck-whipping potholes before Ellery spotted the rough stone wall of the cemetery. He pulled onto the shoulder of the road and parked.

He snapped Watson's leash to his collar, opened the car door, and let the puppy half drag him up the grassy verge to the tall iron gates. The night air was cool, and he could taste the salt in the sea breeze. Watson lunged in an effort to investigate every moonlit flower and shiny rock.

"Take it easy," Ellery told him. "There's no rush."

Watson disagreed. As far as Watson was concerned, there was always a rush. He reached the gates and stood on his hind legs, peering through the bars.

"Yeah, you're pretty cute," Ellery admitted.

He had wondered if the gates might be locked, with an exception made for the Masquerade ghost hunt, but no. They opened on surprisingly well-oiled hinges.

Watson and Ellery slipped through, and Ellery studied the garden of mossy gravestones and tilting crosses and weathered stone figures.

They didn't make cemeteries like this anymore. Nowadays it was all about speed and space. Back in the day, housing the dead had been a gracious and elegant effort. Also occasionally over-the-top ostentatious. Some of these tombstones were taller than him.

The ground was so soft, the footprints of Saturday night's ghost hunters were still visible. That must have made it fun for CSI.

Trees rustled to his left, and Ellery's head snapped toward the noise. Watson let out a startlingly deep growl and began to tug at his leash. Ellery pointed his phone's flashlight in the direction of the whispering leaves. Eyes gleamed in the darkness.

The hair rose on his nape. But unless they were being hunted by someone only a foot high—or crawling on their hands and knees—Ellery was pretty sure it was another dog.

He let out a long breath. "No, Watson. Leave it alone."

The better part of Ellery's acting career had been spent in graveyards—the real thing and movie sets alike—but there was definitely something about this place.

Or maybe it was the knowledge that someone had been murdered in that mini temple on the hill.

Watson muttered unpleasant observations about critters who lurked in shrubberies, but allowed Ellery to lead him away.

The ground beneath their feet seemed to vibrate with the steady crash of the surf against the cliffs. The night was loud with crickets singing their sea chanteys—and an owl heckling them from the trees.

Was this a bad idea?

Jack would probably think it was a bad idea.

But then Ellery disagreed with Jack about a lot of things Jack thought were a bad idea.

Anyway, it wasn't like this was a bad part of town. A dead part of town, maybe. But not particularly dangerous. The last time anyone had been mugged on Buck Island was way back before Jack had been police chief.

A little voice in the back of his head whispered, *They don't waste time on muggings here. They jump straight to murder.*

Oh-kay. He did not want to start thinking those kinds of thoughts.

Thinking of Jack had dampened his enthusiasm. He missed Jack. He missed their previous friendship. But Jack had offered an olive branch yesterday evening. Maybe more than an olive branch.

"I'm not saying this out of jealousy."

Of all the interesting things Jack had said, that had to be the *most* interesting.

On impulse he pulled his cell out and pressed Jack's number. After all, it was only smart to make sure someone knew where he was, just in case.

It took several rings, enough that Ellery checked the time and blinked. Midnight. Yikes. He had been thinking it was still around nine. Jack was probably sl—

"'Lo?" Jack's voice was thick with sleep. He cleared his throat, rasped, "Chief Carson."

"*Hey.*" Ellery lowered his voice and then wondered why. "I woke you. I'm sorry. I didn't realize what time it was."

"Whmm-hmm Ih Ih…" Jack mumbled. It sounded like he dropped the phone in the bedclothes—or maybe a bucket of water.

"Sorry? What?"

Jack swore, there came some mighty rustling sounds, bedsprings pinging, and then Jack's voice came on crisp and clear. "I asked what time it was, but I can see for myself. Where'd you break down this time?"

"I didn't."

"You didn't? I see." The funny thing was, Jack didn't sound irritated or impatient or suspicious. He sounded…almost amused. "Ah. Game night is over, I guess?"

"Yes…" Ellery was distracted by Watson trying to wriggle out of his harness, a new and unwelcome trick he'd picked up on their last walk. "*Stop it,*" he whispered.

Watson gave him a you-talkin'-to-me? look.

"What?" Jack asked.

"Just clearing my throat."

"Did you have a good time? Are you still hanging onto your winning streak?"

"Yeah. That is, no. I—" Wait. Wait. Wait. Was Jack *chitchatting* with him? At midnight? Because that was not part of their dynamic. Their friendship was not the call-you-up-just-to-talk variety. Let alone call-you-up-just-to-talk-at-midnight. Typically, their phone conversations revolved around topics like finishing nails, wood sanders, and stay-out-of-my-crime-scene.

"Are you home now?"

What if I'm not? What if I said I was parked down the street? Would you ask me to come over?

Ellery thrust that thought from his mind. Just because Jack was in a chatty mood, just because his voice was slightly drowsy and warm and sort of... affectionate, just because Jack was kind-of-sort-of sounding like a boyfriend, was no reason to jump overboard. Jack had been as clear as a guy could be that he did not want a relationship.

No way was Ellery making *that* mistake again.

"Not exactly," Ellery said.

Maybe Ellery's tone sounded funny because Jack's tone also sounded funny—and interested—as he said, "No? Where are you? Are you still in Pirate's Cove?"

"Sort of." Ellery admitted, "I'm at the cemetery."

"You're…"

"Want to go ghost-hunting?"

"Tell me you're kidding." Jack did not sound at all soft and sleepy and affectionate now. He sounded wide awake and alarmed.

"I'm kidding about you wanting to go ghost-hunting, yes. But I have a theory."

"So do I," Jack said grimly.

"Did you know that Tom Blood was the one with the idea to build the tunnels beneath Pirate's Cove?"

"What in hell—"

Ellery hurried on. "It occurred to me that there must be an underground passage from the Blood-worth house to the mausoleum."

"It occurred to me too," Jack said. "So I *asked* Marguerite. There was a tunnel at one time, but it collapsed."

Ellery absorbed that.

"Maybe she's lying."

"That also occurred to me. She's not lying. She showed me the collapsed tunnel. There isn't any way through. I saw for myself."

If Ellery were honest, he'd have to admit he was a little disappointed Jack had already thought of the underground-tunnel idea—not to mention, dispensed with it. Granted, it wasn't an original idea, not on Buck Island.

Ellery quoted, "'When you have eliminated the impossible, whatever remains, however improbable, must be the truth.'"

"Thank you, Mr. Holmes. I used to read detective fiction too, remember?" Jack sounded less exasperated and more resigned. "How much did you have to drink tonight?"

"Two drinks. I left early so I could check out my theory."

"I bet. Well, your theory is a bust. Why don't you come over, and I'll make you a cup of coffee for the drive home?"

The drive home was twenty minutes, give or take, but it was an offer Ellery couldn't refuse—sadly, because he didn't want to.

He sighed. "Okay. I'll be there in ten—oh *hell*." Ellery yelled, "WATSON!" as Watson, after some consideration, had given a full-body shrug and slipped right out of his harness.

Finding himself unexpectedly free, Watson took off like a shot, a black shadow racing toward the trees blocking the view of the cliffs and the ocean below.

"I've got to go," Ellery said. "Watson's loose." He clicked off, pushed his phone into his pocket, put his fingers to his lips, and whistled.

Watson looked over his shoulder, muzzle open in what sure as heck looked like a huge grin, slowed to a lope, doubled back...and proceeded to run rings around Ellery.

Literally rings. The puppy ran in large circles, zigzagging through tombstones and urns, speeding by just out of arm's reach at regular intervals.

"What the heck's gotten into you?" Ellery demanded as Watson zipped past him yet again.

Watson laughed soundlessly, disappearing around another pedestal.

"Okay, that's it," Ellery called after three more minutes of failed grabs at the puppy drive-by. "I'm leaving. You can grab a cab."

He started back toward the entrance, watching to see if Watson followed. In the past, this trick always worked.

Tonight? Not so much.

Instead, Watson took off in the opposite direction, galloping up the hill, barking at whatever psychotic visions were dancing in his head.

Arf! Arf! Arf!

Ellery groaned. *"Really?"*

Arf! Arf! Arf!

Yes. Really.

CHAPTER SEVENTEEN

Unhappily, apologetically, Ellery picked his way through the graves and tombs, trying to find the actual path.

Arf. Arf. Arf.

Let's hope he doesn't wake the neighbors.

It felt like forever, but it could only have been another minute or two before Ellery located the stone path leading up to the Bloodworth mausoleum.

Watson's bark echoed in the distance.

God, don't let him fall off the cliffs.

That horrific image electrified Ellery, and he sprinted up the hill, reaching the top, out of breath, heart pounding.

The marble mausoleum gleamed in the moonlight, the narrow faces of the half-hidden angels watching slyly from their niches.

He whistled again and then jumped as Watson suddenly burst out of the mountain of wild roses behind the back of the building, greeting Ellery like a long-lost comrade.

Ellery's heart melted, though he knew this was supposed to be a teaching moment. For which of them, he wasn't sure.

"Yeah, yeah. It's obedience school for you, buddy. Or maybe the bomb squad." Weak with relief—and doing an obstacle course in less than a minute, Ellery snapped Watson's leash on his collar, trying to avoid, unsuccessfully, Watson's enthusiastic, wet kisses.

For a moment, he studied the mausoleum.

There was no police tape across the entrance. Did that mean the crime scene had already been cleared?

"If you twist the head of the mermaid on the ship's figurehead, it releases the spring..."

It couldn't hurt to try? Since he was already here? Just to check for himself.

Not that he didn't believe Jack about the tunnel being sealed off. He did. Marguerite, on the other hand...

Ellery approached the marble door, studying the carvings of ocean waves and sea serpents.

Which way had Julian twisted the mermaid's head?

Ellery twisted clockwise.

Nothing.

He twisted counterclockwise.

The door seemed to shudder, and then the slab of stone rolled back with a hair-raising scrape of stone on stone, a sound familiar to anyone who'd ever watched a mummy movie.

Yes.

It really was that simple.

Ellery gave a disbelieving laugh. He glanced down at Watson.

Watson wagged his tail, looking up at him.

"What do you think?"

Watson brightened. He thought what he always thought. *Game on!*

"Come on."

The puppy trotted into the chamber, and Ellery followed. His flashlight beam played around the interior, spotlighting the faded jewel tones of the painted ceiling, the glittering eyes of gleaming statues covered in gold leaf, the dizzying swirl of the blue and green tile mosaic floor.

His impression on Saturday night that the mausoleum itself did not contain sarcophaguses, tombs, or coffins, was correct. However, the far wall was a columbarium with decorative niches for urns. Most of the niches were empty.

That meant there would have to be a way down to the crypt where the eighteenth century Bloodworths were entombed. All available real estate below must have been used up, which was why the more modern-looking columbarium had been added. No room at the zoo.

But there was no obvious entrance to the lower chamber.

He turned his attention to the columbarium. The ceiling-high structure seemed to consist of three panels: the left half of the columbarium, then a central panel with a long inscription carved into stone, and then the right half of the columbarium.

It was easy to believe the structure had been designed to preserve the large and clearly older inscription, but Ellery couldn't help noticing that the panel with the inscription was door-shaped.

That fit with his theory.

Except there was no hillside or cave or anything built behind the mausoleum, so even if there had been a door, where would it lead to? There was a thicket-sized rosebush, but how did that help? Or was that the point? Did this support Marguerite's statement that there had been a tunnel at one time, but a cave-in had closed it off?

Maybe. Except architecturally, it still didn't make sense to have a door there.

Maybe it wasn't a door.

Maybe the inscription itself was the clue?

Slowly, Ellery read the inscription aloud. "'Instead of the laughter of men, the singing gull. Instead of the drinking of mead, storms there beat the stony cliffs, where the tern spoke.'"

Okay, then.

What did it mean? There were caves in the cliffs overlooking the ocean all along this coastline. Was this a reference to that? Maybe there was a passage leading to a cave in the cliffs? That might have been useful in Captain Blood's time, but did it have any relevance now?

Sometimes a poem was just a poem.

Was that the case here?

He was distracted from his thoughts as Watson strained at his leash, sniffing mightily at the large, asymmetrical ink stain spreading from the corner of the far wall. Ellery's stomach retreated to his throat.

Dried blood. A lot of dried blood. Dried blood spray on the wall. Dried blood spread on the floor. From the size of that ominous human-sized stain, Brett had been killed inside the mausoleum.

That eliminated one theory: that Brett had died somewhere else and his body had been hidden in the tomb to delay discovery. In that scenario, someone would probably have arranged things to look as though Brett had left the island of his own free will.

But that had not happened. If Brett had been killed in the mausoleum, something else must have been going on.

Maybe there wasn't a plan. Maybe the murder had not been premeditated. Maybe Brett had opened the mausoleum himself, opened the door to his murderer.

That didn't prove Brett's murderer wasn't a member of the family, but it did open up other possibilities. Brett's killer might not have known the secret to opening the mausoleum.

Or they might have.

Julian hadn't tried to hide how to open the mausoleum from Ellery. It seemed safe to assume that a number of non-family members knew the way through that forbidding stone door.

He swung the flashlight beam toward the entrance. Something on the tiled floor glinted in the ray of light.

Ellery bent down and picked up…a spoon.

A very small sterling silver spoon. A demitasse spoon?

Now that was truly weird. Weird in itself, sure, but also weird that the police would have missed it in their crime-scene investigation.

Not just weird. Impossible to believe.

But if the police had not missed it, then the spoon had been dropped *after* the crime scene had been cleared.

Which meant—

Ellery sensed a strangeness in the air, something hard to pinpoint. Motion? Movement? Watson gave another of those unnerving guttural growls. His huff rose as he stared past Ellery. Ellery looked around, nearly overbalancing as he swung the light. The flashlight beam illuminated a nightmarish vision.

Someone—some *thing*—stood over him. It was *right there*. Ellery's horrified gaze took in a mask-white face with a long beak and soulless black eyes…

The curtain dropped.

* * * * *

Kisses.

Wet, sloppy, frantic kisses. A whining that hurt his ears.

He tried to pry his eyes open. Too painful. No point. He couldn't see anything.

More kisses. More whining. Puppy breath…

* * * * *

"Ellery?"

He knew that voice.

Once again he tried to open his eyes. His lashes weighed a million pounds. It hurt to move them. He struggled to unstick them, lash by lash…

A blinding light stabbed at his eyes. He winced. Closed them tight.

Jack's voice reverberated down a long tunnel…a secret passage…

"Ellery? Can you hear me?"

Poor Jack. He sounded frightened. Frightened and angry. Ellery wanted to answer. Wanted to tell Jack it was okay. But he was so tired. The light was so bright, and Jack's voice was so far away.

He closed his eyes.

* * * * *

That smell.

He knew that smell. What was it?

Disinfectant. But not just disinfectant. Chemicals. Cleaning fluids. Other fluids. Nothing good. That smell never meant anything good.

Hospital smell. That was it.

Ellery frowned, opened his eyes. Blue walls, generic framed photos of the pier at Pirate's Cove, an IV pole. Yes, a hospital bed. In a hospital room. The bent and battered blinds on the window seemed to squint at the early morning light filtering through. On the other side of a beige curtain divider, someone was snoring up a storm.

What the...?

He hadn't had a headache like this since...ever. He put a cautious hand to his head and felt a goose-egg-sized lump.

"Oh, you're awake!"

He turned his head cautiously.

She was young. Late twenties? Blonde ponytail, huge hazel eyes, anorexically thin in powder-blue scrubs. "How are you feeling?"

"Is that a trick question?" Ellery croaked.

"If you can joke, you must be feeling better." She smiled. "I'm Daisy. Would you like some water?"

Yes. Definitely. His mouth felt like a blanket that had been wrapped in mothballs for the last twenty years. "Thanks."

He struggled to sit up, and Daisy said, "No, no. Let the bed do the work."

She hit a button, and the top half of the bed rose into reclining position. "How's that? Better?"

"Yeah." A lot better. He felt so dizzy. How could you feel dizzy sitting?

Daisy handed Ellery water in a plastic cup.

His hand shook as he gulped it down. It was the best thing he'd ever drunk, although he felt slightly sick afterward. His head was thumping, and he felt disturbingly woozy.

"What happened to me?"

"Well…" Daisy hesitated. "It's normal to have some blank spaces. I should probably get Dr. Mane."

That was fine with Ellery. He closed his eyes.

The fourth time Ellery opened his eyes, he found himself gazing up at Todd.

He smiled into Todd's smiley green eyes. "Hey," he said softly. "Long time no see."

Todd's eyes widened. "Hey," he said in a breath of minty-fresh.

Abruptly Ellery remembered that Todd did not have smiley green eyes, that he and Todd had broken up months ago, and, most importantly, this was not Todd.

"*Oh,*" he said. "Sorry."

"Why?" the guy with the green eyes asked with interest.

He was clearly a doctor—white coat, stethoscope, expensive watch, which he was checking in between glances at Ellery—and Ellery realized he was in the Buck Island Med Center, that it was afternoon, and that something had happened to him. Something he could not quite remember.

He also could not fail to notice that this doctor was really attractive. Tall, nicely built, and a little older than himself. He had curly blond hair, chiseled features, and, yes, smiley green eyes.

Also yes, he did look disconcertingly like Todd, but only at certain angles. He was better-looking than Todd.

"Why am I here?" Ellery asked. "What happened to me?"

"I'm Dr. Mane, and you're at Buck Island Med Center." Dr. Mane drew up a small rolling stool and sat down. "How are you feeling?" His smile was sympathetic, as though he knew exactly how Ellery was feeling.

"Confused."

"That's normal. How's the headache?"

"It's there," Ellery admitted, which was an understatement.

"Ringing in your ears?"

"A little."

Dr. Mane glanced back at the half-closed window blinds. "Does the light bother your eyes?"

Ellery said again, "A little."

"Are you feeling a little queasy maybe? A little nauseous?"

"Three out of three," Ellery said.

Dr. Mane smiled faintly. "That's all normal with concussion."

Ellery's unease grew. "How would I get a concussion?"

"You don't remember?"

"No."

"Do you remember—"

Ellery cut in. "I remember my name, I remember my address, I remember what year it is, who's president, I remember everyth—" He gulped as memory flooded back. "Where's Watson? Where's my dog?"

Dr. Mane looked apologetic. "I'm not sure about your dog. I can try to find out."

"He was probably with me when I— Did I have a car accident?"

"No."

"Did I fall off a ladder?"

Dr. Mane looked intrigued. "Do you fall off ladders a lot?"

"No. Not a lot."

"Good. You'll want to stay off ladders for a while. But no. The police chief found you in the old cemetery at Seal Point. You were unconscious." He watched Ellery closely.

"In the *cemetery*?"

Dr. Mane nodded.

"Was I— How did— Why would I—"

Dr. Mane didn't answer.

Ellery turned this news over in his mind. Any way he looked at it, it did not make sense.

He said slowly, "I was unconscious? Do you mean I hit my head, or did someone knock me out?"

"It's unclear at this point."

This was bewildering. Ellery protested, "I don't remember anything. None of this makes sense."

"Okay, well, that's not a problem," Dr. Mane said quickly, easily. "You have a mild concussion, so some confusion is to be expected. The memory loss is probably temporary. There's nothing worrying on your CT scan, and no reason you shouldn't make a full recovery."

Ellery nodded, winced, said, "Thank you."

"Thank your creator for giving you an industrial-strength noggin." Dr. Mane offered another glimpse of his very nice smile.

Ellery tried to smile back. He was suddenly very tired.

"We're going to keep you here overnight again," Dr. Mane said, "but you can probably go home tomorrow. "How's that sound?"

"Great. Thank you." He blinked at Dr. Mane. It was all he could do to keep his eyes open.

Dr. Mane patted Ellery's knee and rose. "Get some rest. That's the most important thing. You'll be feeling better in no time."

Define "no time."

But yes, Ellery did feel somewhat better when he woke later that afternoon. That was partly because he had been dreaming that he was chasing Watson through the old cemetery at Seal Point, and he suddenly came face-to-face with Brett Ainsley. The covered-in-blood, animated corpse of Brett Ainsley.

He gulped in air to yell—and woke up.

Shadowy sunlight striped the wall and photos across from the bed, a lot of people were talking loudly in a nearby hallway, and a lot of people were talking loudly on the other side of the dividing curtain.

"Aunt Martha is baking you a welcome-home cake right this very minute," a way too cheerful voice was saying.

Ellery's stomach did an unhappy list and roll.

"You okay?" Jack asked.

Jack?

Ellery jerked his head—yes, it really was Jack sitting next to his bed—winced, and said, "That depends. Are you going to yell at me?"

"Not until you're feeling better."

"Then no, I'm not feeling better."

That was a lie, though, because just the sight of Jack, sitting there straight and stoic in his navy uniform, was like a shot in the arm. Ellery felt instantly more awake, more alert, more alive.

Jack's smile didn't reach his eyes. In fact, his eyes looked like they had faded to gray. Maybe that was the dim light of the hospital cubicle, but he did look very tired.

"You look better," Jack said. "Better than you did last night, that's for sure."

Ellery smiled, but it was a lackluster effort.

Jack considered him, said, "I was going to try to smuggle Watson in, but that bark." He shook his head. "We'd never make it past the reception area."

"He's with you?" The surge of relief almost swamped Ellery. "You've got Watson?"

"Yep. He's staying with me until you're up and around. He's over at the station right now, asking for his lawyer. Loudly."

"Thank God." Ellery laughed, then put his hand to his head. "Ouch."

"Yeah." Jack sighed. "If you're up to it, I need to ask you about last night. Dr. Mane tells me you might have some gaps in your memory."

"Last night is one of them."

"Last night? The entire night?"

Ellery started to nod, then thought better of it. "Yeah. Sorry."

"What's the last thing you remember?"

Ellery half closed his eyes, trying to recall. He said at last, "Dylan has a new girlfriend."

Jack's brows rose. "I thought he and Janet were...?"

"He says they're just friends."

"Mm. Okay. Then you remember game night? Do you remember leaving Dylan's house?"

"The conversation with Dylan was earlier in the day. At the Crow's Nest. I don't remember much after that. I don't remember game night."

"You don't? Do you remember talking with me on the phone?"

"No." Ellery studied Jack's face. "Did I call you? Or did you call me?"

"You phoned me. You were at the cemetery, and you asked if I wanted to go ghost-hunting."

"*What?* I must have already been hit over the head."

Jack laughed. "I doubt it."

"Ghost-hunting. That makes zero sense."

"I'm pretty sure you were kidding about hunting for ghosts. I think you went there looking for a secret passage into the Bloodworth mausoleum."

Ellery sat up. "*Yes.* That's it. That's right. I thought there must be a tunnel from the house to the mausoleum because the mausoleum wasn't used as a mausoleum until the early 1900s."

Jack pushed the button on the arm of the hospital bed. The top half of the bed rose, propping Ellery up. "And you were right about that. Except during Prohibition, a cave-in closed off the tunnel. So that's not how Brett or his killer got down to the mausoleum."

"Oh." Ellery slumped back in disappointment.

Jack studied him, said, "It was a good guess."

Ellery made a face. "If you're worried about my feelings, I must be dying."

Jack grinned, shook his head. "I care about your feelings. I just care more about your skull. You've been knocked senseless twice in the little time I've known you."

"No way. The first time I was just stunned. And I did that to myself."

"I've been a police officer for ten years, and I've never been knocked unconscious."

"U R Doin it Wrong," Ellery said, and Jack snorted.

It was good to see Jack looking more relaxed, smiling at him. Good to hear the warmth in his voice again, the hint of teasing. It would have been nice if Jack had come ghost-hunting—not least because Ellery wouldn't have been hit over the head.

Jack's gaze grew quizzical. "Are you falling asleep?"

"No. No." Ellery smothered a yawn. "I don't know why I'm so tired."

"It's called concussion."

"Oh yeah." He smiled at Jack, and Jack smiled back with the funniest, sweetest expression. A look Ellery had never seen on Jack's face.

Maybe he was already asleep and dreaming? Because this was—

Ellery's eyes flew open. He started to sit up again, but this time Jack planted a hand on his shoulder, holding him in place.

Jack said, "Ellery, will you please relax?"

"I just thought of something. Whoever attacked me had to be the murderer."

"Not necessarily."

"And it wasn't Julian. Julian has an alibi." The relief was enormous. Not just because he liked Julian. He was relieved to be off the hook of proving Julian innocent. The weight of that responsibility had been smothering.

Jack looked so carefully and completely blank, Ellery felt a flash of alarm. "What?"

Jack hesitated, which was not like Jack.

"No?"

Jack said reluctantly, "Julian doesn't have an alibi. Marguerite pulled some strings at the State House, and he was released on bond yesterday evening."

Ellery opened his mouth, but he had no idea what to say. It was like getting hit over the head again.

The beige curtain divider slid open with a scrape of rings on metal.

"How's my favorite patient?" Dr. Mane asked.

Ellery smiled—it was kind of impossible not to smile at Dr. Mane.

"Great," Ellery lied. "I was hoping maybe I could go home this evening."

"Mm." Dr. Mane was regretful. "Tomorrow at the earliest. That was a pretty good conk on the head. We need to monitor you for at least another night."

"Yeah, but—"

"I know. Believe me. But better safe than sorry." Dr. Mane seemed to belatedly notice Jack. "Chief Carson. Nice to see you again."

"Dr. Mane." Jack rose.

Dr. Mane looked apologetic. "Sorry to interrupt. This won't take long."

"That's okay." Jack was already moving around the bed and heading toward the door. "I should be going."

Ellery swallowed his disappointment. "Tell Watson I said hi."

Without glancing round, Jack put a hand up in farewell and kept walking.

CHAPTER EIGHTEEN

Ellery had been hoping—expecting—to hear from Julian, but it was Nora who phoned that evening.

"Now, dearie, you don't need to worry about anything. I've spoken to Libby and Felix, and they're both willing to work at the Crow's Nest until you're back on your feet."

"What? No!" Ellery said. "We can't afford another employee. Let alone two. Anyway, I'm on my feet now." At least, he had been for as long as it took to get to the restroom and back. He was currently in bed, and grateful to be there.

Still.

"No. No. No."

Maybe there was an issue with the normally reliable island communication system, because Nora did not appear to hear him.

"It's not really *two* employees. Libby will take the morning shift, and Felix will take the afternoon shift. There will be two little hours where their shifts overlap, so that I can have my lunch."

Nora did not take a two-hour lunch, but Ellery did not miss the point that it was not fair to expect her to run the bookshop by herself.

"Nora, there's no need. I'm getting out tomorrow. If you're not comfortable on your own, let's close the shop for the day, and I'll be back on Thursday."

Nora said seriously, "You won't, you know. Concussions are tricky things. You have to give yourself time to recover. I know what I'm talking about. I fell off Mohegan Rock when I was twenty. I was in bed for a month."

"You..."

"You're going to be out of commission for at least a week, dearie. Mark my words. We have to have some help, and this is the perfect solution."

"Is it? I thought Libby and Felix broke up." As soon as the words were out of his mouth, Ellery felt confused. *Were* they? He couldn't remember where he'd heard that.

Nora made a dismissive noise. "They just need a little time and privacy to work things out."

"A little time and privacy working at the Crow's Nest? Oh no. *Please* tell me you're not trying to play matchmaker."

"What nonsense is this?" Nora sounded ever so slightly piqued. "They're babies. I wouldn't think of trying to *matchmake*. Peace-make, yes. They certainly can't be mortal enemies and perform together in the Scallywags."

Was it concussion making him feel like his head was spinning? Or just an overdose of Nora?

"Right. Okay."

"The funeral is Friday."

"Whose funeral?" Ellery asked blankly.

"Brett Ainsley's funeral." Nora sounded concerned. "You do remember that Julian Bloodworth was arrested for Brett Ainsley's murder?"

"Yes. Of course."

"Marguerite has asked Chief Carson for permission to go back to New York with Julian after the funeral. Or perhaps you didn't know that Julian was released on bail?"

"I knew." Ellery slowly digested this news. On the whole, he thought he was relieved. The fact that Julian hadn't contacted him, was seemingly headed back to New York, surely meant that he considered Ellery off the hook as far as proving his innocence?

Nora mused, "I do hope they're not going to try to make a run for it."

"Marguerite and Julian?"

"Yes."

"Marguerite and Julian might make a run for it? You mean flee the country? Why would they do something so stupid?"

"Presumably because they each believe the other is guilty."

Ellery put a hand to his head. "I'm not following this at all."

"It seems obvious to me."

"Do you know for a fact that Marguerite suspects Julian? And vice versa?"

"No, no. I'm just speculating out loud. We have a new theory."

"We do? I mean, we who?"

"The Silver Sleuths, dearie." Nora's voice grew warm with concern. "You poor child. You really are quite befuddled. And no wonder. Look at the time. You should be asleep."

"Wait. Nora—"

"Now you get some rest, and we'll talk tomorrow after they spring you."

"Wait!" Ellery said. "What's the new theory regarding Brett's murder?"

Nora chirped, "I'm sure you've already considered it. We can discuss tom—"

"WHO?" Ellery demanded.

"What's going on over there?" a querulous voice called from behind the beige curtain. "Some of us are trying to sleep!"

"Who?" Ellery hissed.

Nora hissed back, "Locke Lombard, of course," and hung up.

Perhaps the Silver Sleuths had it right.

Ellery's Wednesday morning breakfast tray arrived with the news that Locke Lombard had confessed to the murder of Brett Ainsley and surrendered himself to the police.

Ellery's petition for a copy of the *Scuttlebutt Weekly* was denied. His appeal brought Dr. Mane, looking both amused and regretful.

"Here I was thinking Chief Carson was joking when he said you were some kind of amateur sleuth."

"He *was* joking," Ellery said. "But I know these people. I have some…involvement."

"Well, sure," Dr. Mane said. "It's an island. We all know each other—or of each other. But the thing is, you've suffered a concussion. That's a brain injury. In your case, the injury appears to be mild, but symptoms can manifest even several days after the traumatic event."

"I know. I run a mystery bookstore. Ninety percent of injuries suffered by characters in mysteries are concussions."

Dr. Mane laughed, although Ellery was being serious.

"Sure, but it's not like in the books or in movies. Your brain needs time to heal, which can take seven to fourteen days. Ten is the average."

"Ten *days*?" Ellery gaped at him.

"On average. It takes however long it takes. Right now, you're still experiencing a number of symptoms, so you are in no way ready to return to work. I'm not one hundred percent sure you're ready to be discharged."

"Don't even joke," Ellery said.

Dr. Mane spread his hands in an I-don't-make-the-rules. But then he said, "Honestly, we don't have the bed space to keep you. If you'll promise to obey the following rules—and these are rules, not guidelines—I'll sign your release papers."

"Deal. Er, I promise."

"You haven't heard what I'm about to tell you."

Ellery opened his mouth, but Dr. Mane said, "One. You're not cleared to return to work until the twenty-ninth."

"That's two weeks!"

"If you come in for your check-up on the twenty-fourth, I might give you the all-clear then."

"You know," Ellery said, "I don't actually need your permission."

Dr. Mane gave him that very charming smile. "True. But you're a smart guy—though maybe a little peculiar. I'm betting you're too smart to ignore your doctor's orders."

Ellery scowled. "What's the next rule?"

"Daisy will give you the full list of Dos and Don'ts, but basically, take it easy for the next couple of weeks. Avoid activities that require a lot of concentration or focus. Avoid bright lights and loud sounds. Don't drive—in particular, do not drive to work. Limit your screen time. *Do not* play any sports or climb any ladders—"

"Climb any ladders?" echoed Ellery.

Dr. Mane's mouth twitched. "Rest whenever you feel like it. Stay hydrated. Eat plenty of protein, especially foods rich in Omega-3s, antioxidants—"

"Did you say *I* was peculiar?" Ellery asked.

Dr. Mane grinned, but said only, "Do you have someone who can stay with you?"

Ellery stared in alarm. He said quickly, "Um, yes. My roommate Watson."

"I thought Watson was your dog?"

Ellery blinked.

Dr. Mane tapped his temple. "Yep. I'm paying attention." He considered for a moment or two. "See who you can round up to stay with you. I'd hate to have to call you every three hours tonight. What would we talk about?"

Ellery studied him uncertainly. In other circumstances, he'd be wondering if... He glanced at Mane's left hand. No wedding band.

Maybe yes. Maybe no. Hard to tell.

Mane raised his brows in inquiry.

Ellery said, "I'll phone a friend."

Mane nodded in approval. "I'll see about signing those discharge papers." He reached for the divider curtain, glanced back at Ellery—and winked.

Ten o'clock rolled around, and there was still no sign of Dr. Mane or the promised discharge papers.

Ten-thirty came and went, and Ellery began to feel trapped.

He wanted his own home and his own bed. The Buck Island Med Center was a busy, noisy place during the summer months. How anyone could sleep for more than an hour at a time—even without being woken to make sure they hadn't died of concussion—was a puzzle.

Just past eleven, Jack phoned.

"Are you getting discharged today?"

"That's the rumor."

"Did you need a ride? I can't get away, but I could send Martin to drive you home."

That was a kind and unexpected gesture. Ellery was touched.

"Thanks, but that's okay. Felix is supposed to pick me up as soon as I'm cleared for takeoff."

"Okay. You want me to drop off Watson this evening, or did you need a little time to get your bearings?"

"No, no. Bring him home. I miss the little monster."

He could hear Jack's smile. "It's likewise, I promise you."

"Jack, is it true Locke Lombard confessed to killing Brett?"

Jack's tone changed. "Yes."

"But...why?"

"Why did he confess, or why does he claim he killed Brett?"

"Both?" Ellery said slowly, "Then you don't think he did it?"

"No. I don't." Crisp and uncompromising.

"But why would he confess?"

"I think he's throwing himself on his sword."

"I don't follow." As the implications sank in, Ellery's spirits deflated. "You still think Julian killed Brett?"

"I do. I'm sorry. Nothing else makes sense."

"Yeah, but Julian killing Brett doesn't make sense either. I know you believe Julian is unstable, but even so. He'd have to have some reason."

Jack said patiently, "Motive is the most interesting aspect of any crime, but—believe it or not—it's the least important when putting your case together. I think the scene between Brett and Klementina was the last straw for Julian. There was already long-standing animosity between him and Brett. In fact, he admitted to punching Brett after they went outside following the altercation with Klementina."

"Then you don't think the murder was premeditated? But how would he get Brett down to the mausoleum? Because if the scene with Klementina was the final straw—"

Jack doggedly kept ticking off his reasons. "Of our three principals, Julian is the only one who could have made it down to the cemetery and back in time for the firework display. Lombard is in good shape, but he's not in that kind of shape. Julian had easy access to the murder weapon. Lombard did not. In my opinion, Julian stage-managed the discovery of Brett's body in an attempt to use you as an alibi, and he deliberately handled the weapon when the two of you entered the mausoleum, in order to account for any gunshot residue, DNA, or prints that he might have left at the scene."

"But, Jack, that's all circumstantial."

"Just because the case is circumstantial doesn't mean it's not enough to convince a jury."

True. Although, according to Jack, juries preferred forensic evidence. The more, the better.

Ellery said, "Maybe that's all correct, but the more I think about it, the more I believe he was truly shocked when we found the body."

Jack was still being patient, even kind. "If anyone should know that there is such a thing as acting, it's you."

There was no answer to that because it was true.

Into Ellery's silence, Jack said, "I'm sorry. I know you— I know there was something— I know you liked—like—Julian." It was not like Jack to stumble over his words. "I like him too, but I have to follow the facts, and the facts lead to Julian."

"Then why would Locke confess? If it's not going to do any good, I don't understand what you mean about throwing himself on his sword."

"It's no secret that Lombard has been in love with Marguerite for the last twenty years. Maybe he thinks an obvious effort to save Julian will help his cause."

"That's pretty cynical." Also not very practical. How would a prison sentence equal a Happy Ever After for Locke? Except...maybe Locke was counting on not being convicted.

Again, Jack sounded oddly kind, oddly careful. "I don't mean it to be cynical. I'm not saying the gesture is calculated on Lombard's part. I think he genuinely loves Marguerite and would do anything to make her happy. And Julian not going to prison would make her very happy."

Ellery sighed. He was very tired all of a sudden. Maybe he could work in a nap before Felix arrived.

Jack said, "You shouldn't be worrying about any of this. What time did you want me to bring Watson home this evening?"

"Whatever is convenient."

"How about six?"

"Six is great." Ellery smiled faintly, picturing the reunion with his loudmouthed but loveable little buddy. "And thanks, Jack."

"You don't have to thank me," Jack said. "I'll see you then."

CHAPTER NINETEEN

"**N**ora is an interfering old busybody," Libby informed Ellery when she arrived in Tom Tulley's truck to pick him up a little after two o'clock.

"That's pretty harsh." Ellery hoisted himself into the passenger side of the truck. Not that it should have required hoisting—Tom's truck was an ordinary pickup, not a monster truck—but Ellery found he was disturbingly weak and shaky.

Libby threw him a quick, apologetic look. "I don't mean about sending me to come and get you. I'm happy to. It's *why* she sent me."

"Is it because of Felix? I thought he probably wouldn't want to come after everything that's happened." It was a depressing thought.

"Huh?" Libby's eyes were wide with astonishment. "No way. Of course not. It wasn't your fault. Even Felix isn't *that* stupid."

"Are you sure? Because he's kept his distance ever since Skull House."

"He's distant with everyone. He's distant with *me*," Libby said bitterly. "And I get it. He's sad. I'm sad too. But shouldn't it be different between *us*? I thought we were a team. I thought we were—" She broke off to jam the stick shift into gear. The truck engine roared, the vehicle lunged back and then forward, and Ellery hoped a little bit of whiplash wasn't a problem with a concussion.

"Sorry," Libby muttered. She shifted gears again, and they were off, bouncing over the parking lot speed bumps with a fine disregard for all the signs urging SLOW and CAUTION.

"Either way, thanks for coming," Ellery told her. "I couldn't wait to get out of there."

"I know," Libby said. "I hate hospitals. And I'm happy to help. Really. But the only reason she sent *me* is she's mad about Ned hanging around the store."

Now there was an unwelcome thought. "Is Ned hanging around the Crow's Nest?"

"No. He's just waiting for my breaks. But because he and Felix almost got into it yesterday, Nora is suddenly declaring martial law."

Ellery said uneasily, "He and Felix almost got into it?"

"It was Felix who started it. Not Ned." She said fiercely, "*Felix* doesn't know what he wants."

"What happened?"

"*Nothing.* Mr. Carter came and broke it up."

"Mr. Carter…came…and…broke…it…up…"

"It wasn't a big deal. They were outside by then anyway. It's not like they were going to break any-thing, although the way Nora was carrying on..." Libby sniffed, sounding eerily like Nora at her most disapproving.

Ellery said, "I think maybe we should head into the village. I actually feel fine. And I can talk to Nora."

Libby laughed. "I was standing right there when the nurse said you're supposed to go straight home and go to bed."

"Yeah, and I will, but I think we could swing by—"

"Thanks, but no thanks. I've already had one lecture from Nora today!"

They were both silent for the next few minutes as the truck flew down the wide country lane, Ellery wincing as they plowed through the random potholes. Libby, face set, drove like she was trying out for stunt driver on the set of *Mad Max*.

"Everyone makes assumptions about Ned. They don't even give him a chance," she muttered.

"What does Ned do?" Ellery asked.

"He's in a band. He's a musician."

"Ah. What kind of music do they play?"

"Psychedelic pop. Like the Glass Animals."

"Really? That's cool."

Libby said, "It's *very* cool, and Ned is a *very* cool person. He has a day job, but that's all it is."

"Right. What's his day job?"

"He works for Mr. Samms at the Peevish Pig."

The Peevish Pig had been around for twenty years, but was still referred to as the "new" butcher shop in the village.

"Does he like working there?"

"Nobody likes their day job." Libby shifted down as they started the rise to Captain's Seat, and the sunlight flooding through the windshield flashed off her bracelets. One bracelet in particular.

Ellery considered those sparkling black stones. What were those? Black Onyx? They looked as brilliant as sapphires. The setting was engraved and looked like silver. Most of the bracelets Libby wore were tiny beaded things or leather wraps with crystals and quartz. This bracelet was different. It looked heavy and old. It looked valuable.

A prickle of unease ran down his spine.

"That's pretty."

Libby glanced over in inquiry, then followed his gaze to her bracelet. She smiled. "It's an antique. It belonged to Ned's great-grandmother."

"Is it serious between you two?" Ellery asked slowly. If Ned was giving her expensive bracelets, maybe Tom had reason to be alarmed.

"Maybe," she said shortly, and he knew that tone of defiance was not for him, but for everyone who was telling her Ned was bad news.

The rest of the drive passed quickly and in silence, and before long, Libby was circling the drive before Captain's Seat.

Ellery had been expecting to see his battered VW sitting in the drive, but there was no sign of it.

"Where's my car?"

Libby looked surprised. "I don't know. I'm sure no one would steal it."

She pulled to a neat stop before the front steps.

"Safe and sound." She glanced at Ellery, did a double take. "Gosh, you look sick. Are you okay?"

"Yeah." Ellery opened the cab door and cautiously climbed down. "I'm just tired."

"You want me to come in with you?"

"No."

"I could make you a cup of tea."

He smiled. Shook his head. Libby was a good kid. "No, I'm fine."

"Okay," she said doubtfully. "Are you sure?"

"I'm sure."

"Well, see you later."

Ellery raised a hand in farewell, then slowly climbed the steps, letting himself into the house.

It was strangely, sadly quiet with no Watson to run circles around him, yipping and whining his feelings on every subject known to dog. Ellery was very glad Jack was going to drop the pup off that evening. Glad too that he was going to see Jack—though he was trying not to make too much of that.

As he walked down the freshly painted hall, he considered inviting Jack to dinner, but as much as he liked that idea, he really didn't feel up to cooking. Or eating. More than anything, he wanted to lie down and think.

A cup of tea sounded good, though.

He made his way into the kitchen. Everything looked exactly as it had when he'd left the house Monday morning—which felt like a year ago. Luckily for the hastily rinsed dishes in the sink, it had not been a year.

Slowly, he set about filling the teakettle, getting a mug out of the cupboard, checking that the milk in the fridge was still good.

While he went automatically through the motions, he tried to reassure himself that he was worrying about nothing.

There was no reason this Ned kid shouldn't have had a great-grandmother who bequeathed him a beautiful, valuable piece of jewelry. Anyway, the bracelet might not be valuable. To the naked eye, good costume jewelry could easily pass for something more expensive. You didn't have to be familiar with costume departments to know that.

And yes, the Peevish Pig made their deliveries in a white van, but the van had a sour-faced pig logo emblazoned on the side panel. The van he had seen at the Barbys' had no logo, no markings. Granted, the logo could have been hidden somehow. Taped over with butcher's paper?

"You're letting your imagination run away with you." His voice sounded loud in the empty kitchen.

If the kid did use the van for deliveries, he might be familiar with a lot of homes on the island, familiar with who was in residence and who wasn't, familiar with which places had cameras and security systems.

"You're jumping to conclusions."

Yes. He was. And he was starting to talk to himself, a sure sign he had been living alone too long. He was making a lot of assumptions based on the simple fact that Libby had been wearing an expensive-looking bracelet.

The teakettle whistled, startling him out of his reflections. Ellery rose, poured the boiling water into the mug, dipped the tea bag, opened the counter drawer, and pulled out a teaspoon.

Just an ordinary teaspoon.

He stared at it, stared at it, stared…and suddenly he was back in the Bloodworth mausoleum, holding a tiny silver spoon, studying the distinct seaflower pattern in the weird flickering light.

Memory flooded back in a sickening rush. He smelled Watson's damp fur, the ocean, the unnatural, dry, dusty scent of time stopped in its tracks. He felt again his confusion and then the shock as the significance of that spoon in that place sank in; he remembered Watson's deep warning growl, and the horror of looking up to see that thing standing over him.

He closed his eyes, feeling light-headed.

That thing. He—his attacker—had been wearing Brett's mask. The *Medico della Peste.*

Of course. It all made sense now.

Well, no.

But a lot of it made sense now.

He pulled his phone out and pressed Jack's number.

It went straight to message.

He hung up. Tried again.

Straight to message.

"Hey," he said, and his voice sounded wobbly and strange. "Can you call me?"

He disconnected, put the phone down, and went over to the table to sit before his legs gave out.

Why the hell was he so shaky?

Oh. Right. Ned Shandy with the candlestick in the mausoleum. Or maybe it had been a wrench. Or a lead pipe. He was just grateful it hadn't been a revolver.

It could have been a revolver.

But no. Because the revolver had been left at the scene. Because Brett had brought the revolver.

His cell phone rang, jolting him out of his thoughts, and he snatched it up.

"What's wrong?" Jack's voice was hard and anxious. Ready for action, a missile asking for a guidance system.

"I remember. And I know who did it."

"You remember who hit you?"

"No. Yes, that too. I know who killed Brett. And it wasn't Julian. I'm sure it wasn't."

"Ellery—"

"I can prove it. Well, no. I can't prove it. But I think I can convince you."

Jack said patiently, "Listen to me. We'll talk this evening. I promise. Right now you should be resting, and I should be in a meet—"

"Who found me? In the mausoleum. Was that you?"

"Yes."

When Jack didn't continue, Ellery asked, "What happened?"

Jack let out a long breath. "Forty-five minutes went by, you didn't show, and—this will sound strange, but I started thinking I could hear Watson howling. I went looking for you." His voice changed. "You were in the mausoleum, covered in blood."

Poor Jack. That must have been truly awful. Until then, Ellery hadn't considered Jack's feelings.

"Was there a spoon anywhere?"

"A spoon?" Jack repeated doubtfully.

"A small silver spoon. With a tiny seaflower on the handle. I think they're called demitasse spoons."

"I didn't notice any spoon."

"Are you sure? Because there *was* a spoon."

"I didn't see a spoon. I didn't look for a spoon."

"But you see the significance of the spoon, right? CSI must have cleared the mausoleum after Brett's murder, so the spoon was dropped afterward."

After a moment, Jack said, "Are you sure you saw a spoon? Are you sure you didn't—"

"Dream it? No. I didn't dream a spoon. I did not hallucinate a spoon. Jack, in those burglaries, was one of the stolen items a heavy silver bracelet with black gemstones?"

Jack said slowly, "I'm not sure. Why?"

"Libby came to pick me up from the med center. She was wearing what looked to me like an expensive piece of jewelry. I asked her about it, and she said Ned Shandy gave it to her. That he told her it belonged to his great-grandmother."

"Hang on," Jack said curtly, and put Ellery on hold.

Ellery impatiently held on through several perky *Did you know?* public-service announcements.

Jack came back on the line. "Mrs. Lyman forgot to put her jewelry case away after she finished dressing for the masquerade. Among the stolen items was a 1920s silver bracelet with black diamonds."

Ellery felt both relieved and shaken by this confirmation. "I knew it."

"Even if you're right and our thieves have been storing their loot in the Bloodworth mausoleum, I'm not sure why you've jumped to the conclusion that Ned Shandy killed Brett. Why would he? Unless you think Brett walked in on them that night? And they killed him to—"

"No! No," Ellery broke in. "Don't you see? *Brett* was behind the burglaries. Brett was the mastermind."

"Whoa. Slow down."

"No, but hear me out. Whoever was orchestrating these burglaries knew what he was doing. They were well planned. They were organized. That's not the work of teenaged hooligans. They had a van. They had a plan."

"Okay. But—"

"I'm sure you know Brett has a history of petty crime. I'm sure you know he forged a couple of checks last year? Well, that means he needed money—and he wasn't afraid to bend the rules to get it. Who better than Brett would know which of the Bloodworths' wealthy summer friends and neighbors would be home, which homes would have security systems, who possessed the kinds of valuables easily transported and easily liquidated? How else would they get the idea of using the Bloodworth mausoleum to hide the stuff they stole?"

"We don't know yet that they—"

"Yes, we do. That spoon is a dead giveaway."

Jack said slowly, "You do remember that the Bloodworths were one of the first houses to be hit?"

"What better way to throw off suspicion?" Ellery added, "You said yourself they didn't lose much."

"I'm not saying it couldn't have happened like that, but—"

"*Plus*, Brett would have been the one carrying the weapon. It was Marguerite's gun. So Brett. Not Ned. I don't think Ned went there looking for a fight."

Jack didn't argue. Didn't say anything.

"Whatever happened that night, I don't think it was premeditated."

Jack said suddenly, "What exactly did you say to Libby? When you were asking her about the bracelet."

"Not much. I said it was pretty. She volunteered the information that Ned had given it to her."

"Did you question her at all? Indicate in any way you thought it was stolen?"

"No."

"She's a smart girl, though. She might start wondering herself. I don't want her confronting Shandy. I think I'll bring him in again for questioning now."

"Then you think I might be right?"

"I think you might be onto something, yes," Jack admitted.

"It makes a lot more sense, if you think about it. The idea that Julian could run down to the graveyard, shoot Brett and not get any blood on his clothes, then run back in time for the firework show…"

"There were difficulties with the timeline. Yes."

"Plus, it makes more sense that the murder was *not* premeditated. That there was some kind of altercation when Brett went down to the mausoleum to examine the evening's haul. He was so drunk and so belligerent. He was ready to pick a fight with anyone."

"It could have happened that way." Jack was neutral.

"I mean, there really wasn't a viable motive for Julian to have killed him. Not then, not there, not like that. Not with his mother's own gun."

"Okay, okay," Jack said. "You've made your point. Several times over."

Ellery bit back a smile at Jack's tone. He said, "I mean, it's just a theory."

Jack snorted. He said, "I don't need to tell you not to discuss this theory with anyone."

"No. You don't. Who would I talk to? You've got my Watson. Literally."

On cue, a shrill puppy voice in the background began to yap.

Arf. Arf. Arf.

Jack groaned. "You just had to summon the demon, didn't you?"

Ellery laughed. All at once he felt a whole lot better. About everything.

"I've got to go," Jack said. "I'll see you this evening."

"It's a date."

He regretted the words as soon as they were out of his mouth, but Jack said lightly, "Yes. It is."

CHAPTER TWENTY

Ellery finished applying sunscreen, settled his Ray-Bans more comfortably on his nose, and leaned back into the lounge chair recently purchased from Target and now comfortably positioned on the back terrace of Captain's Seat.

The doorbell had rung twice while he had slowly undressed, located his swim trunks, and painstakingly donned them. (He had discovered that if he kept his neck straight and his head very still, the thumping in his skull remained at a tolerable level.) The first time the bell rang, it had been the Garden Isles florist delivering a gorgeous bouquet of roses and honeysuckle, sent with wishes for a speedy recovery from the Scallywags. The second time the bell rang, it had been the Enchanted Island florist, with a giant bundle of sunflowers and more good wishes from the Silver Sleuths.

Not that Ellery wanted flowers from Julian, but it did seem odd that he had not heard a word since Sunday morning. Julian had been so attentive the night of the Marauder's Masquerade—and on the day after, so insistent only Ellery could help him—that this prolonged and distinct silence was confusing.

He did not have Julian's phone number, but it wouldn't be difficult to hunt it down, so the lack of communication was partly Ellery's fault. It was just that Julian was so intense, so emotional. Ellery wanted to wait until he could give him definite good news, but the radio silence was making him uncomfortable. It was like waiting for the other shoe to drop. He hoped Julian wasn't going to do anything impulsive—like flee the country.

The sun was warm and soothing; also soothing was the summer's day lullaby of humming bees and squawking gulls. Ellery's eyelids grew heavier and heavier. It had been impossible to sleep well at the med center, but it was so quiet out here in the middle of nowhere...

A shadow fell across him. Ellery jerked awake.

Julian stood at the end of the lounge chair, gazing down at him. He wore fashionably ripped jeans and a crimson Cthulhu T-shirt. He looked pale, his eyes red-rimmed. "I came to say goodbye."

Ellery sat up too fast, his head swam, and he had to take a minute.

Julian's voice was strained and husky. "I appreciate that you wanted to help, but the case is closed. Locke has confessed. My mother and I are leaving for New York after the funeral."

"Wait," Ellery said.

Julian's gaze was reproachful. "There isn't anything to wait for. I wish you had told me at the beginning that you and Chief Carson were together. You let me make a fool of myself."

"We're not together," Ellery said. "I don't know what you're talking about."

Julian's face twisted in scorn. "Oh please. It's obvious from the way he talks about you. I can't see why you would lie about it."

"Neither can I. Which should prove I'm not lying."

Julian rolled his eyes and turned away. "Good-bye. Have a nice life."

"Wait a minute." Ellery stood up—and then sat back down. "You need to listen to what I have to say. You owe me that much."

Julian's face quivered. "How do I owe you anything? I *loved* you."

Ellery let out a long breath. "First of all, no. You did not love me. You barely know me. We had one date. Maybe you loved the idea of me, but not *me*. No. Secondly, you asked me to help you, and that's what I tried to do. I want you to hear what I found out—at least, what I can share of what I found out—seeing that what I got out of it was a concussion."

Julian glowered. "That was your own fault."

Ellery gaped at him—and then laughed. "Maybe you're right. Anyway, what I want you to know is your mother didn't kill Brett."

Julian seemed to turn to stone. He said finally, between stiff lips, "Why would you say that?"

"Because it's true. She did not kill Brett."

"Of course she didn't! I never thought she did."

"Oh yes you did," Ellery said. "Which is why after we found Brett, you went back into that tomb—er, mausoleum—and picked up the gun. You weren't covering for yourself; you were covering for *her*. You were afraid the scene with Kezzie was the last straw. And I'm sure you've heard the rumors about...before."

Julian's smile was odd. "You mean the rumor that she killed my father?"

Ellery cleared his throat. "That. Yes."

"You really don't know much about anything, do you?"

"I know that your feelings are hurt—mistakenly—and you're being a jerk about it. I also know that your mother is not the kind of woman who would leave her own gun at the scene of the crime."

Julian's eyes narrowed.

"But when we found Brett, you recognized the gun as hers, and you jumped to the wrong conclusion. So you made sure to handle the pistol."

"I was in shock."

"Give me a break. You're not dumb. You deliberately went back in there and did whatever you had to in order to divert suspicion from her."

"Locke killed Brett," Julian said stubbornly. "It makes perfect sense."

"No. It makes no sense. Why on earth would he? How would that help anyone—especially him? Is your mother going to marry Locke now that Brett is out of the way?"

"Not if I have anything to say about it."

Yikes.

"So, no. No chance. Locke confessed because he's also afraid your mother committed murder—and that there's no way she'll let you take the blame for her actions. He's in love with her—really in love—and he's willing to do whatever it takes to save her. Except she doesn't *need* saving. And if she did, she'd save herself—and more efficiently than either of you two could."

Julian spluttered, "I don't know how you think you know so much!"

"I'm an actor. Or used to be. I spent my formative years observing people and cataloging their reactions for future reference. Look, I've told you all I can. I'm pretty sure there's going to be an arrest this afternoon, and Locke will be released. If you still want to leave Pirate's Cove, leave, but not because you're afraid your mother committed homicide. And if you want to stay, stay, but not because of me. I'm through with romance—although I'm always happy to have another friend."

Julian's smile was derisive. "I bet that's not what you tell Chief Carson."

"Jack and I are friends."

"Maybe. But that's not all you are. I knew it the night of the masquerade. I could feel something was off."

Something was off, all right. But Ellery nobly refrained from saying that.

"Look, all I can tell you is, I appreciated the invitation, and up until the ghost hunt, I was having a good time. I like you, Julian. I think you're an interesting and attractive guy. But I'm not looking for romance, and even if I was, I don't feel we have a lot in common."

"Ha!"

To Ellery's ear, that *"Ha!"* sounded a lot like a hurt little kid, and he said, "But I mean it. I'd like to be friends."

Julian seemed to waver for a moment. He said finally, proudly, "That's your loss," and strode away.

*A*rf. *Arf. Arf.*

Ellery was standing in front of the refrigerator, gazing in consternation at all the food stuffed inside, when he heard the unmistakable sound of homecoming.

Arf. Arf. Arf.

Jack was five minutes early.

Ellery left the kitchen, strode down the hall, and threw open the front door. He was grinning as Watson charged in, nearly bowling him over.

Arf. Arf. Arf.

Watson's piercing bark bounced off the cathedral ceiling and walls.

"I missed you too." Ellery squatted down and was promptly knocked onto his tailbone as Watson threw himself into his arms. "Ouch. Okay, okay. Down, boy."

Between puppy kisses and laughing, he was in danger of knocking himself unconscious again. Jack's boots appeared in his line of vision. Jack scooped Watson up, hooked a hand around Ellery's arm, and lifted him to his feet.

"*You* calm down," he growled at Watson. He turned to Ellery. "And *you*—"

They held gazes. Watson licked Jack's nose, and Jack recoiled, sputtering.

Ellery chuckled. "And me?"

"Have some color in your face again." Jack put Watson, who was wriggling and squirming, on the floor. Watson promptly hopped up and down on his hind legs for Ellery to pick him up.

Jack watched this precarious maneuver with resignation. "Who was it who told you he was going to be ten pounds at most?" he asked when Watson was safely cradled in Ellery's arms.

"Dr. Vincent's nurse."

"Because he's eleven pounds now, and he's still got some growing to do."

"I know. It wasn't a deal breaker." Ellery smiled at Watson, who smiled back. "I hope he wasn't too much trouble."

"Oh no," Jack said. "I didn't need all that sleep anyway."

"Have you eaten? People have been bringing me food all afternoon, if you're hungry."

Jack matched his casual tone. "That would be great. I didn't have time for lunch."

Jack followed Ellery into the kitchen, and told him, "You sit. I'll get the food."

"I'm fine. I just get these flickers of vertigo, but then everything's steady again." He was happy enough to take a seat at the table, though.

He watched Jack moving around the kitchen, putting water in Watson's dish, getting out plates and silverware. But then, Jack had helped him refinish the floors, the counters, and the cabinets, so Jack ought to know his way around.

"Good God." Jack studied the contents of Ellery's refrigerator. "There really *is* a lot of food here. You've got groceries for a month. Plus...how many casseroles?"

"Four. I know. It's enough for a funeral."

Jack muttered something in response to that. "It looks like you have your choice of lasagna, tuna casserole, cheese and potato, and..."

"Seafood casserole," Ellery supplied. "From Mrs. Nelson."

Jack looked impressed. "If Mrs. Nelson baked you her seafood casserole, you know you've arrived."

"There's also a cake and two pies in the butler's pantry."

Jack gave a little shake of his head, glanced at Ellery. "What would you like me to heat up? Or do you want it all buffet-style?"

"I'm not that hungry, to tell the truth. What do you feel like?"

Jack didn't go for that. "Yeah, but you're eating anyway, so the thought of which of these makes you feel the least queasy?"

Ellery considered. "Cheese and potato?"

"Cheese and potato it is."

Ellery had to smile, watching Jack efficiently stepping around Watson as he transferred the cheese-and-potato casserole to the oven, set the timer, got a beer for himself and a glass for Ellery.

"What did you want to drink?"

"Water is great. You don't have to wait on me, Jack. I really am fine."

"Water it is."

"Hey," Ellery said suddenly as the memory of the empty drive came to him. "Is my car still up at the cemetery?"

Jack hesitated. "No."

"Did someone steal it?"

Jack snorted. "No."

"Then…"

"It's being autopsied at Robertson's garage."

"*What?*"

Julian was right. Jack's eyes did very occasionally twinkle. "I'm kidding. It's getting a tune-up."

"But…"

"Consider it an early birthday gift."

"Well, that's an awfully nice gift." Ellery added doubtfully, "Thank you."

This kind of gesture was why his friendship with Jack was so confusing sometimes. Even more confusing because Jack was typically such a straightforward guy.

Jack's smile was wry. "You're welcome."

"You know, none of my recent, er, mishaps, resulted from my car breaking down."

"I know. I'm being proactive here."

"Well, thank you. Again."

Jack seemed faintly amused. "Well, you're welcome. Again."

Nan's cheese-and-potato casserole was delicious from the very first savory bite, which was all Ellery could take before he *had* to ask.

"Well?"

"Well?" Jack glanced around the kitchen as if seeking the latest home improvement.

"You're killing me here. How did it go with Ned?"

His heart sank as Jack grimaced and shook his head. "He confessed."

Then Jack's words sank in. "He— He *confessed*?"

"Yep. It couldn't have taken more than half an hour. I think it was a relief to get it off his chest. He's not a killer. Not by nature."

By circumstance, yes. But maybe that was true of everyone. Jack was right, though. If Ned possessed a murderous instinct, Ellery would also be dead.

"What happened?"

Jack regarded him for a thoughtful moment. "It went down pretty much the way you guessed. Brett showed up drunk and belligerent. He'd already scuffled with Julian, who gave him a black eye."

"Good for Julian."

Jack's look was chiding. "Yeah, well. Brett accused Ned and the others of skimming off the top, which, in fairness, was correct."

Ellery thought of Libby's bracelet. "No honor among thieves?"

"Exactly."

"The other men walked out, which made Brett angrier. Ned stayed to try and reason with him. Brett pulled the gun. Probably to try and scare Ned—which he did. I don't think Brett intended to commit murder any more than Ned did, but they struggled, the weapon discharged..." Jack shrugged.

Watson, sleeping with his head on Ellery's foot, was uttering tiny, muted dream barks. The subdued kitchen lighting gave everything a soft, golden sheen. Ellery studied Jack's face in that gentle light. It was a handsome face, yes, but also a good face, a kind face. A face he would like to keep in his life. Maybe Julian didn't understand the value of friendship. Ellery did.

He asked, "Do you know who the other members of the gang are?"

"Yes. Dougie Hardin and Tip Smith. Local men. All three were on my list of suspects. They're in custody now, and we've recovered a lot of the stolen property from the crypt below the mausoleum."

"So that's it? Case solved?"

Jack's grin was rueful. "Don't let this go to your head, but yes, case solved."

Jack finished his beer, went to the fridge for another.

When he sat down again, he glanced at Ellery's empty plate, and started to rise. "You want another serving?"

"No. Thanks. That was more than enough."

Jack, who was already having a second serving, nodded and returned to his meal. Ellery considered him, and finally had to ask.

"What did you say to Julian that made him think we were…involved?"

Jack met his eyes without self-consciousness. "I told him you were my friend and I didn't appreciate your being dragged into his drama." He added, "Anyway, we are involved."

Ellery smiled. "Define involved."

Jack did not smile. He was serious. "You can define it however you like. I feel that we're involved."

"Friends. Yeah, of course."

"We're more than friends," Jack said.

"I mean, I guess it depends on how you define friends."

Jack repeated, "We're more than friends."

Ellery wasn't sure how to answer because, yes, of course they were more than friends. But they had agreed they would not be more than friends.

Maybe Jack could read his doubt, because he said, "I don't want you to feel that I'm yanking you around."

Ellery said, "I don't think that. But there *is* kind of a push-pull in how you…" It was harder to say than he'd expected, although it was something he'd wanted to say for a long time.

"Treat you?" Jack finished.

"Yeah. Frankly. But you made it pretty clear after Skull House. You're attracted to me and you'd rather not be."

Jack gave a funny laugh. "That's… Yeah."

Ellery shrugged. "That doesn't leave a lot to say."

And yet he couldn't help hoping there *was* more to say.

Jack sighed. "This conversation is not going the way I'd hoped."

"What did you hope for?" The idea that Jack had anticipated some kind of conversation between them was surprising in itself.

Jack was silent, studying Ellery so long and so seriously, Ellery began to feel uncomfortable.

"Can I tell you about Hannah? About the baby?" Jack asked.

Ellery's heart froze, but he heard his voice say calmly, "Of course. You can tell me anything."

"I met Hannah in college. I had no idea I was bisexual until I fell in love with her. And maybe it had to do with Hannah and not me. She was one of those people—you know how you hear how everybody loves so-and-so? Well, in Hannah's case, it was true. You couldn't know her and not love her. She was...special. She was one of a kind. I couldn't imagine my life without her. And then the baby was coming, and I had been thinking I couldn't be happier than I already was, but I was wrong."

Jack's face changed for an instant, but then he had control again. His voice never wavered.

"We were going to name him Harold, for her dad, but we called him Harry. This is the part I don't know how to explain, because he was a baby in a womb, but we had so many plans, and we spent so much time talking to him, joking about him, imagining who he would be... that he was already a little person to us."

Ellery reached for his water glass because his throat locked so tight, he was in danger of strangling.

"Hannah was studying for her master's, and she was driving home from class one night, when some asshole, who was texting when he should have been watching the road, ran a red light and plowed into her car. She was killed instantly. Harry was seven months, and they did everything they could to save him. He made it through the first forty-eight hours, but no."

"Jack... I'm so sorry."

Jack glanced at Ellery, saw everything Ellery could not begin to hide, and he gave a funny smile. "This is why I don't talk about it. It's not easy to hear."

"You can talk about them whenever you want."

"At first you're numb. But that doesn't last. And then the pain is... You don't think you can survive it. You don't *want* to survive it. So you take it one day at a time. You know: let me get through today, and I'll decide about tomorrow, tomorrow." He sighed.

"It's like living with a bullet in your heart. You figure it will kill you eventually—hell, you *rely* on that—but until then you go through the motions of pretending you're still alive. And that's how it is and how you figure it will always be. But then one day you notice the sunrise is beautiful. And one day you enjoy your cup of coffee. And one day something makes you laugh. And finally one evening you look across the room and see a guy having dinner and think, I wonder what he's like."

Ellery swallowed.

"Little by little, day by day, you come back to life. You learn to be happy again. Happy with what you've got."

Jack studied Ellery, said slowly, "You even start wondering if you could love again."

Ellery said nothing. Didn't move a muscle.

"But that's a terrifying thought. Terrifying when you know what it's like to lose everything that matters most to you. The idea of risking the life you've managed to rebuild..." Jack shook his head.

"I understand," Ellery said. And at last he thought he did.

Jack drew on his beer. Set the bottle down. Swallowed. "The problem with that thinking is you're choosing equilibrium over joy."

"If that's what you have to do to get through…"

"Yeah, except you shouldn't be 'getting through' your life, you should be living it. Denying yourself everything that makes for a full life means you're living a half-life."

That made sense to Ellery. He just wasn't sure where Jack was going with this line of reasoning.

Jack said, "I didn't think I could feel so much again. But I do care for you."

"I know." Ellery's smile was self-mocking. "You're attracted to me."

"I am. It's more than that, though. And more and more I find myself wondering, what sense does it makes to refuse to explore what could be, just because I don't know what the future holds? Because I do know for sure that a future where you're not around—because I was too afraid to admit I do have feelings, and I do care, and I would like to see where this goes—is not a future I'm looking forward to."

This was so much more than Ellery had hoped for. Yet at the same time, it was difficult, because how could you know how something might end if you were afraid to ever begin? But having heard how much Jack had suffered in the past, the idea of hurting him, even inadvertently, was daunting.

"It's okay, Jack. I'm not going anywhere."

Jack gave a funny laugh. "See, that's the thing. We're all going somewhere, whether we know it or not. My wake-up call was that invitation from Julian. I've been so preoccupied with what *I* was feeling, what *I* was afraid of, that I forgot you've got fears and feelings too. That you also get lonely sometimes."

"Sure, but it's not like I'm actively looking for anything," Ellery said. It wasn't completely a lie. He wasn't looking for just anything.

"Maybe not, but you deserve...the things we all want, the things we all hope for in our lives. And I'm not the first or only guy on this island to notice that."

Ellery had to think that one through. He said slowly, "When you said you weren't speaking out of jealousy...?"

"I wasn't speaking out of jealousy. The idea that you might get sucked into Julian's emotional whirlpool? Not okay. Not on my watch." Jack's smile twisted. "But just because I wasn't motivated by jealousy doesn't mean I wasn't jealous."

Ellery blinked.

Hard to say who rose first, but all at once they were standing in each other's arms and Watson was blinking sleepily, rudely tipped from his slumbers, trying to make sense of what he was seeing.

Jack's first kiss was careful, almost apologetic—a light, warm brushing of lips on lips—and Ellery's answering kiss was reassuringly receptive. Jack kissed him again, not so lightly, and a lot more warmly. Sparks danced before Ellery's eyes.

"I didn't think this was going to happen," Ellery said. He did not mean the kiss. They had kissed before.

"I did," Jack said, and he also did not mean the kiss. "The first night I saw you at the Salty Dog."

Ellery laughed. "Where do we go from here?"

"Hmm…" Jack raised his eyes ceilingward, which could have meant he was giving it some thought—or suggesting Ellery's bedroom—then said, "If my crime-fiction-reading past serves me, you're supposed to have someone staying with you to check on you every couple of hours during the night."

"Yeah, but that's pretty much a crime-fiction thing."

"Is it?"

Ellery asked slowly, "Are you asking to stay the night?"

"Yes."

"To wake me up every few hours."

"Sure."

"And that's it? You're just going to wake me up every couple of hours and tell me to go back to sleep?"

Once before he'd seen that slow, sweet smile from Jack. "I guess we'll find out when I wake you up."

SCANDAL AT THE SALTY DOG

SECRETS AND SCRABBLE BOOK FOUR

MYSTERY STALKS THE COBBLED STREETS OF PIRATE'S COVE

Who or what is haunting recluse Juliet Blackwell, what does it have to do with mysterious goings-on at the Salty Dog Pub—and why is any of it mystery bookshop owner Ellery Page's problem?

According to sometimes boyfriend Police Chief Jack Carson, it's not Ellery's problem, and he should stop asking awkward questions before it's too late.

Ellery couldn't agree more, but it's hard to say no when someone is as frightened as old Mrs. Blackwell. She insists the ghost of long dead pirate Rufus Blackwell has come to avenge himself on the last member of his treacherous clan.

Before Ellery can say, "Yikes!" Mrs. Blackwell takes a tumble down the grand staircase of her spooky mansion, and it's up to Ellery to find who is trying to kill his eccentric customer.

AUTHOR'S NOTE

Dear Reader,

Welcome back to Pirate's Cove, where sinister secrets are buried deeper than Mrs. McGillicuddy's tulips. But also, we never run out of cupcakes! *Mystery at the Masquerade* is the third book in my M/M cozy mystery series Secrets and Scrabble. As with all cozy mysteries, there is no on-screen violence or sex. (I DON'T MAKE THE RULES, I JUST REGARD THEM AS AN ARTISTIC CHALLENGE.)

You may have noticed there is no COVID-19 in Pirate's Cove. You're welcome.

According to the rules of the game (by *game*, I mean the cozy genre, not Scrabble), the stories are quick, light, and fun. This may not be your cup of tea, but in these trying times, I find myself turning more and more often to the reassuring comfort of (okay, yes, frequent) murder in a world where justice always prevails, good will triumphs, and love will *usually* find a way. If that sounds good to you, come shelter in place with me for an hour or two; let today's storm pass us by.

These stories are set on fictional Buck Island. The character of Watson is based on my own adopted pup Spenser (formerly known as Watson).

Thank you a million-billion times over to Keren. Thank you to Kevin for keeping the home fires burning and for understanding that your partner in crime needs to disappear into a world of fantasy for months at a time—and for welcoming me back when I resurface.

Thank YOU, dear readers. Please, please be smart and play it safe.

TIPSY MERMAID MARTINI

INGREDIENTS

- 1 oz Cake Vodka
- 1 oz Watermelon Pucker
- 1 oz Blue Curacao
- Splash of cranberry juice
- Crushed ice

DIRECTIONS

- Fill cocktail shaker halfway with crushed ice.
- Pour ingredients over ice.
- Shake, shake, shake.
- Pour liquid into martini glass.

ABOUT THE AUTHOR

Author of over ninety titles of classic Male/Male fiction featuring twisty mystery, kickass adventure, and unapologetic man-on-man romance, JOSH LANYON's work has been translated into twelve languages. Her FBI thriller *Fair Game* was the first Male/Male title to be published by Harlequin Mondadori, then the largest romance publisher in Italy. *Stranger on the Shore* (Harper Collins Italia) was the first M/M title to be published in print. In 2016 *Fatal Shadows* placed #5 in Japan's annual Boy Love novel list (the first and only title by a foreign author to place on the list). The Adrien English series was awarded the All Time Favorite Couple by the Goodreads M/M Romance Group. In 2019, *Fatal Shadows* became the first LGBTQ mobile game created by Moments: Choose Your Story.

She is an Eppie Award winner, a four-time Lambda Literary Award finalist (twice for Gay Mystery), An Edgar nominee, and the first ever recipient of the Goodreads All Time Favorite M/M Author award.

Josh is married and lives in Southern California.

Find other Josh Lanyon titles at www.joshlanyon.com, and follow Josh on Twitter, Facebook, Goodreads, Instagram and Tumblr.

For extras and exclusives, join Josh on Patreon.

ALSO BY JOSH LANYON

NOVELS

The ADRIEN ENGLISH Mysteries
Fatal Shadows • *A Dangerous Thing* • *The Hell You Say*
Death of a Pirate King • *The Dark Tide*
Stranger Things Have Happened • *So This is Christmas* •

The HOLMES & MORIARITY Mysteries
Somebody Killed His Editor • *All She Wrote*
The Boy with the Painful Tattoo • *In Other Words...Murder*

The ALL'S FAIR Series
Fair Game • *Fair Play* • *Fair Chance*

The ART OF MURDER Series
The Mermaid Murders •*The Monet Murders*
The Magician Murders • *The Monuments Men Murders*

BEDKNOBS AND BROOMSTICKS
Mainly by Moonlight • *I Buried a Witch*

The SECRETS AND SCRABBLE Series
Murder at Pirate's Cove • *Secret at Skull House*
Secret at Skull House • *Mystery at the Masquerade*

OTHER NOVELS

This Rough Magic • The Ghost Wore Yellow Socks
Mexican Heat (with Laura Baumbach) • Strange Fortune
Come Unto These Yellow Sands • Stranger on the Shore
Winter Kill • Jefferson Blythe, Esquire
Murder in Pastel • The Curse of the Blue Scarab
The Ghost Had an Early Check-out
Murder Takes the High Road • Séance on a Summer's Night

NOVELLAS

The DANGEROUS GROUND Series

Dangerous Ground • Old Poison • Blood Heat
Dead Run • Kick Start • Blind Side

OTHER NOVELLAS

Cards on the Table • The Dark Farewell • The Dark Horse
The Darkling Thrush • The Dickens with Love
I Spy Something Bloody • I Spy Something Wicked
I Spy Something Christmas • In a Dark Wood
The Parting Glass • Snowball in Hell • Mummy Dearest
Don't Look Back • A Ghost of a Chance
Lovers and Other Strangers • Out of the Blue
A Vintage Affair • Lone Star (in Men Under the Mistletoe)
Green Glass Beads (in Irregulars) • Blood Red Butterfly
Everything I Know • Baby, It's Cold (in Comfort and Joy)
A Case of Christmas • Murder Between the Pages
Slay Ride • Stranger in the House

SHORT STORIES

A Limited Engagement • The French Have a Word for It
In Sunshine or In Shadow • Until We Meet Once More
Icecapade (in His for the Holidays) • Perfect Day
Heart Trouble • Other People's Weddings (Petit Mort)
Slings and Arrows (Petit Mort)
Sort of Stranger Than Fiction (Petit Mort)
Critic's Choice (Petit Mort) • Just Desserts (Petit Mort)
In Plain Sight • Wedding Favors • Wizard's Moon
Fade to Black • Night Watch • Plenty of Fish
Halloween is Murder • The Boy Next Door
Requiem for Mr. Busybody

COLLECTIONS

Short Stories (Vol. 1) • Sweet Spot (the Petit Morts)
Merry Christmas, Darling (Holiday Codas)
Christmas Waltz (Holiday Codas 2) • I Spy...Three Novellas
Dangerous Ground The Complete Series
Dark Horse, White Knight (Two Novellas)
The Adrien English Mysteries Box Set
The Adrien English Mysteries Box Set 2
Male/Male Mystery & Suspense Box Set
Partners in Crime (Three Classic Gay Mystery Novels)
All's Fair Complete Collection